Ladies of Lancaster County:
The Love of a Friend

PATTY STANSELL

WESTBOW®
PRESS
A DIVISION OF THOMAS NELSON
& ZONDERVAN

Copyright © 2015 Patty Stansell.

All rights reserved. No part of this book may be used or reproduced by any means, graphic, electronic, or mechanical, including photocopying, recording, taping or by any information storage retrieval system without the written permission of the publisher except in the case of brief quotations embodied in critical articles and reviews.

Scripture taken from the New King James Version. Copyright © 1979, 1980, 1982 by Thomas Nelson, Inc. Used by permission. All rights reserved.

WestBow Press books may be ordered through booksellers or by contacting:

WestBow Press
A Division of Thomas Nelson & Zondervan
1663 Liberty Drive
Bloomington, IN 47403
www.westbowpress.com
1 (866) 928-1240

Because of the dynamic nature of the Internet, any web addresses or links contained in this book may have changed since publication and may no longer be valid. The views expressed in this work are solely those of the author and do not necessarily reflect the views of the publisher, and the publisher hereby disclaims any responsibility for them.

Any people depicted in stock imagery provided by Thinkstock are models, and such images are being used for illustrative purposes only.
Certain stock imagery © Thinkstock.

ISBN: 978-1-4908-7639-9 (sc)
ISBN: 978-1-4908-7641-2 (hc)
ISBN: 978-1-4908-7640-5 (e)

Library of Congress Control Number: 2015905692

Print information available on the last page.

WestBow Press rev. date: 4/22/2015

Dedication

To and with Jesus' agape love. This dedication goes to my Lord and Savior. Without Him, I could do nothing, and through Him, all things are possible.

I would also like to dedicate this book to Senior Pastor Bob Ortega of Calvary Chapel, Las Cruces, New Mexico, and his lovely wife, Mary. Without the love of Christ and the knowledge that pours forth from Pastor Bob's teaching from the pulpit and from Mary as she teaches the ladies, I would never have had enough knowledge of God's Word to write this book or those to follow.

I am so grateful God led me to you. Thank you both for all the love you have always shown me. God be with you always.

Chapter 1

Lancaster County, Pennsylvania, 1966

Laura woke before dawn. The heat made it hard to sleep. It was warm even though it was still spring. It was her favorite time of year; the trees were all in bloom, and the flowers were putting forth buds, and some were even blossoming. The wisps of air coming through the windows smelled heavenly to her. Laura nestled her face into her pillow, inhaling the smell that can only come from line-dried sheets.

Laura turned sixteen that day, which meant the start of her *rumschpringe*—the Amish period of "running around" for teens. Well, it would start as soon as her parents permitted it, that is. Then she would be attending the singings. For the Old Order Amish, they allowed their teens sixteen and older to go in a group to one of the neighboring barns with refreshments and hay bales sitting around to gather, sing songs and get to know one another. This would be a place where the teens might find a person to court.

Laura remembered when her sister Mary had turned sixteen. It had been Mary's special day with a singing to boot since her birthday had fallen on a Sunday. Laura, being too young to attend, had raised her bedroom window and listened to the fun coming from the barn. Laura, who had been thirteen, had felt just as mature as the others and hadn't understood why she couldn't attend the event.

Sitting in bed, Laura wondered how Mary would be able to get up for the morning chores. Mary had been out with Micah again the previous night and had gotten no more than an hour of sleep, if that. Laura could tell how much Mary loved Micah; it showed on her face every time she looked at him.

Mary and Micah had been attached at the hip, so to speak, since Mary turned sixteen. She had met him at the third singing she had attended. Isaac, Laura's older brother, had taken her. Micah had asked her to ride home in his courting buggy after watching her for three singings.

Micah Miller, along with his family, his Uncle Robert and Aunt Lisa Miller, had moved from Ohio three and a half years earlier. Most Amish men tilled the land, but Micah always loved working with wood and with his hands, which is what his Uncle Robert did for a living.

Back in Ohio, Micah's father, Elmer, had watched his son's shoulders slouching when Micah had tilled. Micah had done the work but had not been happy about it. Elmer had a large family, and it took a lot to feed and care for them. But after the women put up enough for the family, they set aside the rest for Saturday markets. They could always count on the bounty to make ends meet.

Since childhood, Micah had always carved on wood. His father had watched Micah's smile spread from ear to ear as he finished one project after another. He had made small wooden wagons, trucks, and such things for his siblings for gifts. Elmer knew woodworking was in his son's blood and had let Micah move to Lancaster County to learn from the best, his brother, Robert.

Rebeka Knapp, Laura and Mary's *mamm*, went past the door and tapped it lightly. "Girls, it is time to get up."

Laura, startled from her wandering thoughts, said, "Be right down, Mamm." Laura's thoughts of Micah and what she had been told about him made her happy for her sister. It would soon be her turn to meet someone nice and hopefully marry at the appropriate age.

"Mary, you awake?" Laura asked, nudging her.

"Jah, I didn't really sleep." Mary sighed. "Trying to remember everything Micah and I talked about kept me from it. My evenings with him mean so much to me, Laura. One day you will understand."

Laura assumed Mary had forgotten her birthday since she didn't mention it. She jumped out of bed and into her work frock and headed downstairs pinning her bun on the way. Just before she reached the bottom of the stairs she put her kapp on her head over her bun. It didn't take long before Mamm told Laura to give the bell a ring, letting their menfolk know it was time to come in for breakfast.

After everyone got washed up and *Daed* was sitting at the head of the table, he asked for all heads to be bowed for the silent prayer. The food was passed around. The full plates and the sound of lip smacking told Mamm all was well with her world. She knew the belching at the end of the meal would be the clincher, signaling they had enjoyed her food. They always had plenty of food; Mamm said the men needed hearty breakfasts as the days were long that time of year.

Just the fact of being Amish meant that the tight-knit family had so many blessings to be grateful for. It took many hands to complete all the chores as well as work the fields, but the large family made the chores fun with their laughter and good-natured teasing. They didn't need electricity for radios or TVs; the Amish and some Mennonites thought that electricity interfered with what God intended for them to do.

The one day of rest was the Lord's Day, a day the Amish did not allow manual labor. All the food eaten on the Lord's Day needed to be prepared the day before. Usually, Laura and her family ate cold cuts, cheeses, and a variety of side dishes along with homemade breads sending heavenly aromas from each loaf.

After breakfast, Laura noticed her mamm and Mary talking by the sink as Mary washed the dishes. Laura brought the last of the dishes from the table to the sink, and her mamm and Mary got quiet when she got within earshot. Since it was Saturday, market day, and there were always plenty of things to do redd up for the big event, Laura assumed they were talking about market day and let it go.

"Laura, did you finish loading the wagon with those jars of jellies as well as the boxes of handmade items and the quilt?" Mamm inquired.

"Jah, Mamm. Is there anything else for me to do before we head off to town?" Laura asked sweetly. She didn't want to let them know her feelings had been hurt.

Mamm and Mary looked at each other, thinking hard. "No, guess not, so we had better be on our way. We are expecting a very busy day with all the *Englischers* milling around our area," Rebeka said. "This being your last year in school, and with only three weeks to go, I am sure you are excited. After that, you will be staying home with Mary and me, learning how to run a household."

Laura thought that if her mamm had remembered how many weeks were left until school was out, she surely wouldn't have forgotten her birthday.

"With the weather being so warm this year, we don't have to wear our sweaters—but bring them just in case," Rebeka said.

Mamm took the reins. She made sure Debra was seated beside Laura. Mary took her place in the front beside Mamm, and they were off to market.

After unloading the wagon at their normal booth, Laura spotted her best friend, Abby. "Mamm, may I go say hello to Abby?" Laura asked.

"Jah, but don't be gone long. Mary and I have some shopping to do, and you will have to be here to watch the booth and Debra," Mamm said.

"*Denki*, Mamm. I will hurry," Laura said.

Laura tripped as she was running to Abby. "*Ach mei!*" She knew she was going to fall but couldn't stop. Just then, a hand reached out to break her fall. She looked up and saw the bluest eyes and the brightest smile. She didn't know the young man smiling at her. *Who is he?* she asked herself.

"Hello. Glad to have been able to help. Someone as lovely as you need not be picking herself up out of the dust. My name is Jacob Yoder."

"Well hello, Jacob," Laura said, flustered. "I'm Laura Knapp."

"I am here from Ohio, living with my relatives, the Millers. They moved here a few years back. Do you know them?"

Laura knew her face was beet red and her apron and *kapp* askew. Many times her mamm had told her, "Young ladies do not run." As Laura straightened her apron and tightened the pins holding the bun under her *kapp*, Abby showed up to meet her—and none too soon, as Laura was tongue-tied. Never before had someone had that effect on her.

Abby saw Laura's dilemma and spoke up to give her friend time to compose herself. "Happy birthday, Laura. What a beautiful day, don'tcha think?"

Laura shrieked with delight that Abby had remembered her birthday. "Well, denki, Abby!"

"Hello," Abby said to the young man.

Laura had recovered enough to be able to introduce the two. "Abby, this is Jacob Yoder. Jacob, my best friend, Abby."

Jacob said hello to Abby, but his eyes went right back to Laura. Her hair was like spun gold, and her eyes were the color of emeralds, so green he was quickly lost in them. She was the prettiest girl he had ever seen.

"So it is your birthday, is it? Happy birthday, Laura. Now I will never forget the day we met," Jacob said, smiling.

See? Not everyone forgot my birthday. "It was very nice meeting you, Jacob. Denki for rescuing me. It would have been quite a sight, seeing me sprawled out on the ground," Laura said, laughing at herself.

They stared at each other until Abby cleared her throat and said, "Laura, we must be going."

Abby was right—they did need to get going. Her mamm had said not to be gone too long. The girls bid Jacob farewell and left.

"Ach, Abby, did you see how cute he is?" Laura was gushing. "He must have been hiding." Even as flustered as she felt, she remembered he had said he lived with the Millers.

Shocked at Laura's obvious infatuation with the young man, Abby said, "Laura, we're too young to be thinking of boys right now." As always, Abby being the sensible, practical one of the two, wanted to make sure her friend heard her thoughts. "Especially boys we don't know. He isn't even in our order."

Laura listened to Abby ramble. She didn't want to spoil her birthday by fighting over trivial matters, so she kindly said, "Ach Abby, he's living with the Millers. And if you remember, the Millers waited on a letter from their bishop in Ohio, and once it arrived, the ones old enough joined church."

"How long has Jacob been here?" Abby asked again.

"Why are you asking all these questions about Jacob? He was ever so kind to keep me from falling," Laura replied.

"I'm sorry," Abby said. "I'm just a little out of sorts with you for all the attention you were giving him."

"Would you like to visit our booth for a while? I'll go with you to ask your mamm," Laura said as she hugged her friend.

"Ach, I am sure Mamm will be agreeable to it. We have always spent our birthdays together. See you soon," Abby said as she left.

Laura realized Abby was right. The time seemed to have gotten away from her. She knew she should get back, trusting that Abby's mamm would allow her to come.

Laura arrived at the booth and helped finish setting up. There were so many pretty handmade things—a beautiful quilt with stitches so small and so even it looked as though it could have been done on one of the Englischers' sewing machines, plus doilies, dresser scarves, and many other items. The Englischers almost always bought every quilt her mamm brought to sell; her work was well known for miles around.

While they were setting up, Mamm asked Laura, "Where is Abby?"

Laura told her she would be along soon.

When they finished setting up, Rebeka and Mary got ready for their shopping spree. On their way out, she left instructions for Laura. "Make sure you watch your sister and keep an eye on things. Sometimes, these Englischers, especially the younger ones, don't think they should have to pay for things. We won't be long."

As Rebeka and Mary were walking away, Laura saw how close her mamm and Mary were. She wasn't jealous. Actually, she couldn't be happier for her sister; she didn't begrudge the closeness they shared.

As Laura sat at the booth, she looked over their handmade things, and the quality of each piece pleased her. She noticed how well Debra's pieces had come out. Laura's things didn't compare to Mamm's or Mary's. Her mamm told her to keep practicing and she would improve. Perseverance was the key to making every stitch perfect.

Abby came bounding around the back of the booth out of breath, her face glowing with excitement. "I can stay for a while."

The girls were chatting at the booth when Rebeka and Mary stopped by to see how things were selling. At the same time, some Englischers stopped to check things out. Laura got up to take care of the customers, giving Abby a chance to speak with Rebeka just out of earshot from Laura.

"Ach, Abby, it is so gut to see you this morning. Did Laura suspect anything while you spoke this morning?"

"Not a thing, Mrs. Knapp. In fact, I believe she thinks the whole family forgot her birthday," Abby said, grinning.

Laura was busy with an Englischer woman who bought the only quilt Rebeka had made that week. There were many weeks Rebeka would have two quilts for sale. The family would be blessed with the income from the one sold.

"Well, her daed and *brooders* are getting things redd up as we speak for the party this afternoon. Mary and I spent all day yesterday cooking things that would store in the cold house. Now don't forget, you young people need to be at the farm before we arrive to truly surprise Laura," Mrs. Knapp said with a smile.

"Ach mei, she will be so surprised! It's been fun helping you. Of course, I wished her happy birthday or she would have been on to us for sure and for certain," Abby said with a laugh.

Just as they were finishing their conversation, Laura finished with the customers and approached them. She wondered what they had been talking about in such hushed tones. *Hmmm.*

"We need to finish our shopping and stop off and say hello to Martha," Rebeka said. "We won't be gone long, Laura."

Rebeka spotted Martha at her booth and thought of all the years of friendship between Martha, Rachael, and herself. Rebeka hugged her friend. "I just love that girl of yours. She is so gut for Laura. My girl can be a little boy crazy at times. Ach, our girls are growing up so fast," Rebeka said.

"Jah, the girls are close for sure, just as we were. Abby can't stand it each year when Laura turns a year older two weeks before her birthday. Laura loves to tease Abby by saying, 'I am a year older.'" The mothers laughed and hugged one another as they had done for as many years as either could remember.

Rebeka and Mary finished their shopping and returned to the booth. They fixed lunch for everyone, and after lunch, Abby said she had to help her mamm pack things up.

As Abby was almost back to their booth, out popped Jacob Yoder. "Abby, my cousin, Micah Miller, said earlier this morning we would be going to the Knapp's this afternoon. Is Laura's birthday party the reason?"

"Jah, that is correct. I would appreciate you not saying anything to her before the party as it is to be a surprise. Well, I need to go."

"Jah, I will keep it to myself, and I will see you later," Jacob said.

Sometime later, Rebeka and the girls started packing up. "Girls, we need to leave. You know how your daed and brooders are about eating on time."

Laura knew she should not be acting so self-centered about her birthday, but her feelings were hurt; her family hadn't remembered it. But she was determined not to be a baby about it. After all, she was a woman and would act like one.

"So Mamm, did you and Mary get all your shopping done?" Laura asked. She didn't see anything new in among their belongings.

"Jah we did, denki for asking," Rebeka said as she put the last box into the wagon.

The trip home took no time at all. As they turned up their lane, Laura spotted all the buggies lined up by the barn.

"What is going on?" Laura asked.

"We had such a hard time keeping this surprise from you," Rebeka said.

Laura's eyes lit up. "You didn't forget, did you? Oh, hurry Mamm! Hurry!" Laura couldn't hide her excitement.

Laura spotted Abby jumping around with as much excitement as she herself felt. Laura jumped from the wagon, and Abby caught her in a big hug. "Are you surprised? I can't tell you how hard it was not telling you today. We have never kept secrets from one another, and I felt ever so guilty for doing so."

Laura hugged Abby. "What a *wunderbaar gut* day it has turned out to be. After all, where was my faith? My family couldn't forget my turning sixteen!"

"I think you will be happy to know Jacob came with Micah and the rest of the Millers," Abby said. Though she wasn't too happy that Jacob had come, her friend's birthday seemed more important, so she was determined not to spoil Laura's fun.

Laura was so excited. She started pulling Abby along, saying, "Hurry, hurry! I don't want to miss one minute of this party."

Chapter 2

Twice monthly, the Old Order Amish held church, and that Sunday's church was held at the Stoltzfus farm. There were a few in the group, especially Rachael, who felt that every Lord's Day should find them sitting in the pews learning more of God's Word. Their Mennonite neighbors didn't miss a Sunday going to church along with a midweek Bible study. She wondered why they didn't study God's Word more.

Rachael did feel blessed to have a Bible study with Ruthie when she went over there. Ruthie was her first cousin who had moved back to the area a few years earlier. She had missed Ruthie all the years they had been apart and felt grateful for the hours of work she got in each week. Every time the two women opened their Bibles, Rachel hungered even more for God's Word; she never wanted to stop when the time came for the *kinner* to get back to their school lessons. However, she knew Ruthie didn't have more time as she homeschooled her two kinner.

Because Rachael was so ill, Ruthie always felt better about them studying the Bible than with Rachael working. Ruthie was the person that talked Rachael into going to the doctor in the first place and had promised her silence until Rachael was able to convince her husband, Joseph, into going to the doctor with her and listening to what they had to say about her illness. She also would never take any credit if and when Rachael came to saving grace; she knew that was all God's doing. She loved her cousin and wanted the best for Rachael. Ruthie, a Mennonite, knew Rachael must come to know Jesus and have Him in her heart before her passing. Ruthie and her husband, Robert, had kept Rachael's secret of her illness to themselves.

Martha Stoltzfus, Rachael's lifelong friend, finalized the last few items to take to the food table for after the service. She was glad to have Rebeka to share her feelings with this morning. Rebeka was the third one in their trio of friends since childhood.

"It is so gut to see you looking so fresh this morning after the big party for Laura yesterday. She seemed to be having the time of her life. The surprised look on her face said it all. It thrilled Abby being asked to help, ya know. Abby talked about all that went on at the party for most of the evening," Martha told Rebeka. "Rest yourself. I'm almost finished here, and we'll head to the barn. The menfolk must be ready to start the services. You know how Bishop Malachi gets when he is kept waiting. None of us want to get on his bad side." Martha chuckled.

"When we were young, the hours spent on the backless pews didn't seem to bother any of us. However, Aaron's back gets worse with each passing year. I see the pain in his eyes by the end of the service. It makes my heart hurt for him. The three hours it takes for our services does him in. He is starting to gray, both his beard and what hair he has left," Martha said with a laugh.

"We all agree with you. At least the ones our age or older," Rebeka said laughing out loud. "The old adage 'The older one gets, the faster time flies' doesn't count when it comes to the three hours on those backless wooden benches."

"You were such a gut friend after Aaron's accident. Never did I look up from Aaron's hospital bed that you were not there, always praying and encouraging his family and me. The whole community helped on the farm and with his younger siblings. Ach, what a time Aaron went through. With Aaron's back broken, none of the family knew how well he would recuperate or for that matter if he would walk again. To this very day, I give thanks to our heavenly Father every time Aaron is able to walk out the back door to tend to his chores," Martha said.

The ladies headed out the door, their arms loaded. A smile crossed Martha's pretty face. "God will always see us through our trials if we place our trust in Him. I just pray our kinner keep the Scriptures they have been taught next to their hearts. More important, they must heed God's Word and practice it daily."

Rebeka put her load on the table, as did Martha. Rebeka said in a low voice looking right into Martha's eyes, "I truly wish I would have listened to both you and Rachael and shared in your faith. It was harder for me, but then, you know most. As I said yesterday at the party, we have very few things we haven't shared with each other. It is the same for our girls. I am grateful Laura and Abby are so close. Laura inherited her charm for the boys from me. I pray she doesn't get wild during her rumschpringe. I hate to think back to those days," she shared with her friend.

"Well, as I remember it, you went to take care of Kathleen, your sister, during most of your running-around period. When you came back, you met Abraham, and as far as Rachael and I could tell, you didn't have eyes for anyone else. You and Abraham were inseparable and didn't let the grass grow under your feet. You were baptized and wed that same fall," Martha said.

Rebeka's face turned pink. She hoped Martha would attribute it to the heat of the day. She wanted the conversation directed away from her. "I watched Laura at her party. If she didn't have her eyes on Jacob Yoder, he had his on her. I can tell there is an attraction between them."

"Laura is a gut girl. She just likes the boys a little more than she should for her age. She will be starting her rumschpringe as soon as school is out. But Rebeka, I trust Abby and know she will keep Laura as safe as Laura will allow. Abby has a heart for our Lord. She spends time each day in His Word." Martha smiled at Rebeka, trying to reassure her. "I am not trying to say Abby is perfect. We both know better than that. She just has that sweet spirit about her that shows the love for her heavenly Father."

"You are right about Abby having a sweet spirit. However, it is time I contact Kathleen. Not only do I miss my sister something terrible after all these years, but I am sure she can fill me in on Jacob Yoder. You know, she married into the Miller family from Ohio. I believe her husband is a cousin to the Millers down the road. I believe Lisa told me her husband's sister married a Yoder. It will be better to know, and then it can be put to rest."

"Rebeka, you know how many Millers and Yoders are in every Amish and Mennonite district. The names are common, and you need to put aside your worries for the day. After all, this is the day to worship God and have gut fellowship and enjoy the tables full of food together." Martha saw the worried look on Rebeka's face.

The service seemed especially long that Sunday. All the adults were sitting straight, their ears open to the bishop while he read the Bible in High German. For the young ones, it seemed long, and most of the *bobbeli* were sleeping in their mamms' arms. Once the bishop dismissed them, the men started putting the benches back into the wagons.

As soon as that was completed, they gathered at the tables of food. The bishop led them in silent prayer, and once he said amen, the ladies started serving.

The dishes laid out were many. The ladies always made sure there were plenty of pickled beets, an assortment of pickles, and a variety of chutneys along with chowchows. There were cold cuts, cheeses, and salads among many other dishes. After the men and then the children were served, the ladies took their own plates. They had plenty of time for fellowship; no one was in a hurry to pack up and head home. They enjoyed one another's company, and the mamms and mammies spoke of the cute things their kinner and *kinskinner* had done the past two weeks.

After a wonderful afternoon of enjoying each other's company, the ladies cleaned up and took their leave. The only family staying behind was Abraham Knapp's.

Martha and Rebeka were in Martha's kitchen finishing up the dishes. "Rebeka, are you sure you are not just trying to keep Jacob and Laura apart? He has been coming to church with the Miller family ever since he got here. And yes, he is very shy, and that is probably why we haven't gotten the opportunity to get to know him. He is always very quiet and humble. I think you worry for naught."

"You are always so wise, and I do appreciate your counsel. I'll give it some thought," Rebeka said. "Either way, I need to make contact with Kathleen. It has been way to long. It is time to let bygones be bygones."

"I could not help hearing the sorrow in your voice when you spoke of Kathleen earlier. It is only natural to miss her. I know I could never have stayed away from any of my family that long. I never did understand why you two did not stay in touch by letters at least," Martha shrugged. "I know how blessed I feel having my family close. Not to mention how large we have grown in numbers. It is hard to keep track of all those towheads and who they belong to out there. If we were not constantly together, I know I would be lost with the towheads' names.

"We are truly blessed here. Not many are sick with the maple syrup urine disease or the Crigler-Najjar syndrome. It is because we have young people moving into our area. No one seems to be marrying close relatives any more. I can't imagine what it must be like to have to put the babies under the blue lights every day. How very sad it is for those mothers to see what their babes must go through."

"You are right about that. The young men moving into our district are a blessing in disguise. Then there is Paula Miller. She is also from Ohio. She and Lucas will be wed this winter. That also helps to bring in new blood to our district. It seems to have kept the diseases at bay in our area. By the way, when is the frolic to finish Paula's quilt?" Rebeka wanted to know.

"It is over at Ellie's this coming Wednesday. I'm glad you mentioned it. She is one go-getter. Lucas is a lucky man, ya know. Paula bubbles with joy, and her hands fly at the tasks given her." Martha laughed, thinking back to a few frolics she had attended with Paula.

Martha loved her younger sister Ellie and her family, but Barbara, Ellie's middle child, held a special place in her heart. To Martha, Barbara was sunshine on a rainy day. Never did she have anything but a smile for everyone she met. She glowed with love as she entered a room.

"Oh Martha, Barbara is such a sweet girl. Going to Ellie's will double the fun, seeing Barbara and quilting with Paula. Barbie suffered so much as a baby, but look at her now. She lights up a room like the morning sun, and she seems so much older than thirteen."

"Do you remember when she was born and the trials she went through? The doctors didn't give her long to live. However, by the time a year rolled around, she was pulling herself around on the floor. By age two, the doctors said, 'It's a miracle.' But we know where the miracle came from, God alone."

"Didn't they take her to the Mayo Clinic after getting permission from Bishop Malachi?"

"Jah, they did. The physical therapy group helped Jonathan and Ellie work with Barbie. They were wonderful with her. When the doctors couldn't figure out why she wasn't paralyzed with her vertebrae not connected at the bottom of her spine, all they did was shake their heads. There didn't seem to be any real damage to the spinal cord. There just wasn't any way of attaching it without risking paralysis. They explained at that time that Barbie would never stand. Then the doctors tried to convince Jonathan and Ellie they should put Barbie in a home where she could get proper care. I don't believe any of us ever saw Jonathan that upset." Martha shook her head at her memories of that time so many years earlier.

"Well, can you blame him or Ellie for that matter? I couldn't handle the thought of losing one of my kinner. I would have brought my daughter home and cared for her as they did," Rebeka stated.

"He and Ellie packed Barbie's things and brought her home along with a lot of information from the physical therapy group. In that lot of information, a picture of the wheelchair caught Jonathan's attention. Once Jonathan saw the picture of the chair, he lovingly crafted one for her. He knew that as she grew, he would have to build larger ones to fit her. He is such a gut husband to my sister, not to mention what a great daed he is. Ellie feels very blessed she caught his eye at just the right time. Ellie blushes whenever it is brought up. Her face still shines, and it shows how much she truly loves him whenever she looks his way." Martha's smile showed the love she had for all of them.

"Barbie never lets her disability get in the way of what she wants to do. She is so gut with the kinner, all of them," Rebeka said as she watched through the kitchen window at the kinner playing. There sat Barbie with two on her lap, her face aglow with love pouring out for each child.

"Jah, Barbie is very special and has such a sweet spirit about her. She is a big help to Ellie with the twins. She truly enjoys having them with her. I am so proud of her. I know God has something big in store for her."

"Martha, when I hugged Rachael gut-bye earlier, her body felt so frail. Has she said anything to you?" Rebeka was worried.

"Not of late. I know she is still helping Ruthie with cleaning and whatever else she can do. Rachael and Ruthie being close cousins is the only reason Joseph lets her work outside the home. Of course the money is a blessing to them. I would be surprised if Ruthie even lets her work very hard. Ruthie is a kind Mennonite woman and wouldn't think of letting Rachael overdo it," Martha said.

"Rachael hasn't been feeling well for what seems to be years. She can't keep any weight on that small frame of hers. We were all happy when Rachael's mamm and daed moved into the *daadi haus*. Mammi Ingersol comes in every morning to lend a hand getting the morning breakfast done and Allie is also a big help to both of them. She stopped going to school after the eighth grade, as is the norm. I wish we would have stopped Laura and Abby at the end of the eighth grade. It didn't seem to affect Abby as it did Laura," Rebeka said. "That seemed to give Laura another way to meet boys."

"Let's pray the doctors find out what is wrong with Rachael soon. She is so spiritually strong, even through her trials. We must never forget to give God His praise, honor, and glory He so righteously deserves. We all pray, but Rachael seems to have something more spiritual with God, especially lately. She seems to have such a peace about her even as ill as she is. It is as though God is right beside her."

Martha put the last of the dishes into the cupboard. "I have to tell you something." Her eyes were locked on Rebeka's. She lowered her voice so no one could hear. "I have been reading more of the Bible, and I am starting to get a real hunger for His Word. God is ever so faithful when we call upon His name."

"Ach mei! Martha, please be careful. I would hate to lose you or your friendship should the brethren find out," Rebeka said in a pleading voice.

Chapter 3

As Rachael walked along the road leading to her Mennonite cousin's house, she marveled at God's handiwork, the beauty of this earth. *What an artist our heavenly Father is. Just looking at the beauty takes one's breath away*, Rachael thought as she walked along to her cousin's house.

As Rachael approached the house, she realized Robert, Ruthie's husband, wasn't home. Robert, being the community's only vet, used a car to get from one farm to the next. He said it saved him time. He also used a small office in town as a clinic for smaller animals.

A married Amish woman normally didn't work outside the home. But Rachael loved helping Ruthie with the cleaning and the children. Then there always seemed to be time for their study in the Bible, as Ruthie wouldn't let her do much work. For the last several years, she worked for Ruthie on and off. The previous two years, the harvests were not fruitful, which made Rachael all the more thankful for the work.

It seemed so sad to see the crops pushing their heads toward to sun, looking as though they would produce a good crop only for a drought to hit them. Their little heads would wilt and fall to one side. For that reason, Rachael working for Ruthie seemed God's way of letting them eke out a living even when nature challenged them.

The children, Robbie and Ginnie, ran out to meet Rachael. Ruthie and her family had moved back to the community some years earlier, and since the Amish-Mennonite schools were full, Ruthie decided to homeschool them with help from Robert. Robert taught science, history, and the Bible, and Ruthie taught the rest. The children were looking forward to the fall session as the community spoke of building onto the school and finding another teacher.

Ruthie was delighted to be back where she had grown up and to see Rachael once again. With their mamms being sisters, they had spent much time together in their younger years. She watched Rachael walk up the lane. Worry didn't begin to express her feelings for this cousin she loved with every ounce of her being.

Ruthie knew Rachael needed Jesus in her life being as sick as she was. Ruthie spent many hours on her knees with her beloved husband. They prayed diligently for Rachael to come to saving grace.

Rachael entered the house with the children chattering away like little magpies. She couldn't get a word in edgewise. She spent time talking to each child for a few moments and turned to greet their mamm. "Morning, Ruthie. I believe Robbie and Ginnie grow every day. Look how tall Robbie is getting, and Ginnie is not far behind. What are you feeding these two?" Rachael asked while teasing the kinner.

"Rachael, how wonderful it is to see you this morning." Ruthie gave Rachael a gentle hug. "As for those two and Robbie's hollow legs, they eat everything in sight. Being that age, they have a lot of energy."

"I thought I remembered this being your morning break time from teaching. Is that right?" Rachael asked.

"Ach, this is perfect timing. I just released the kinner. Please have a seat, and we can chat over cake and coffee," Ruthie said.

Ruthie brought coffee and cake to the table and went to get her Bible. "I could not ask for a better break than one filled with God's Word. I always feel so refreshed after our study." Ruthie had been praying so hard that Rachael would see the light of Christ in her life before God took her home. Ruthie worried about her. If Rachael accepted Jesus into her heart, Ruthie would know she would see her again someday. She knew how much better she felt knowing her mamm was waiting with Jesus for her to join them.

"I brought the new Bible you gave me. However, for the time being, I should leave it here. I am not ready to explain to Joseph why I have a new Bible or am reading it and accepting the New Testament. I sure did love the Gospel of John. But then, all the first four books in the New Testament tell of His life in their own words.

"When I was looking in Luke and came upon the story where Mary visited Elizabeth and heard her greeting, the Holy Spirit came over her, and the baby she was carrying leaped for joy inside her womb. From that point, Elizabeth knew Mary was carrying their Lord and Savior.

"In the Bible, Jesus tells us we will be with Him if we ask for forgiveness and repent of our sins." Rachael paused. "Ruthie, you talk to Jesus as if He is right here with you. Is that how you feel?"

"Well He is," Ruthie stated with assurance.

The puzzled look on Rachael's face caused Ruthie to take her cousin's hands in hers. She looked into her eyes with a sisterly love. "Jesus says, 'My sheep hear my voice, and I know them, and they know Me.' I am so happy to hear that you read the Gospels. They are the true story of the life of Jesus. It also states in Romans 8:1, 'There is therefore no condemnation to those who are in Christ Jesus, who do not walk according to the flesh, but according to the spirit.' And Romans 8:2 says, 'For the law of the spirit of life in Christ Jesus has made me free from the law of sin and death.'

"So you see, we have Jesus to take our sins away," Ruthie said. "We have the Holy Spirit as our Comforter. Did you get far enough into Acts, where Jesus tells us that when He went to be with the Father, He would then send the Comforter to us? This is why we must always pray in the name of Christ Jesus, and we ask His will be done, not ours. We must always pray to the Father and Son and listen to the Holy Spirit. They are the Trinity. Remember in Genesis where God said, 'Let Us make man in Our image'? He was also referring to His Son and the Holy Spirit."

"I do remember reading that. It is just hard for me to grasp it all. As far as praying to Jesus, I just wish we could pray like you do in my home as a family," Rachael added, "During our silent prayer before meals, I do pray to God to help my husband and children after my passing." Rachael took in a breath so slowly Ruthie began to worry she had stopped breathing. Rachael explained that the pain had caused her to wince. She told Ruthie to wipe that worried look off her precious face; the last thing she wanted was anyone fussing over her. She decided to be truthful with her cousin, who had been there for her for the previous two years.

"The doctors told me at my last appointment that my white blood count was higher than before. My husband doesn't want to hear anything about it. We decided, the doctors and me, at this stage of the cancer, it would not do any good to try any of the more aggressive treatments." Rachael sighed. It seemed that the weight of the world was on her shoulders. She went on.

"I did some reading they gave me about my kind of cancer, and Ruthie, I am so tired. The only true peace I find in my day is when I am reading the Bible you gave me. God's Word gives me the strength and peace to accept this. I say 'this' or 'it' instead of cancer because it makes it easier to cope. I realize God is in control. The hard part is truly relying on Christ alone instead of my own understanding. Jesus is our Lord and Savior, and He is our best friend."

"However, you know that our teachings in the Amish faith, especially the Old Order, taught us not to claim Jesus as our personal Savior, that it was considered arrogant to do so. They also teach us that we won't know we are saved until we stand before God on Judgment Day and He then decides. Arrogance is thinking we can do things in our own flesh. I realize now it is through Jesus that '*All*' things are done through Christ. The Gospel of John opened my eyes. Ruthie, I am ready to say the sinner's prayer. Would you lead me through it?"

"Ach mei! Rachael, it is another prayer answered by God! I would be honored to help you."

After Rachael said the sinner's prayer, Ruthie ended with a prayer of thanksgiving. "Thank You, God. Now I know Rachael will be in heaven awaiting our arrival. Be with her in her time of need. Let her rest in Your arms, Father, and ease her pain. She is now Your child, Father, just as You always knew she would be, Amen."

Ruthie had kept Rachael's secret; Ruthie knew Rachel needed someone to confide in. Rachael told Ruthie she knew she would need to share that with Robert, her husband. Ruthie wanted Robert to speak with Joseph for Rachael; she didn't think they could reach him.

However, she knew all things were possible through Christ, so she would not give up on him because God wouldn't.

Robert came driving up just as Rachael readied herself to head home. Confessing with her mouth to God and accepting Christ as her Lord and Savior had given her such joy, but it had worn her out. They both thought Rachael should go and rest at home.

After greeting his wife with a hug and a kiss, he turned and hugged Rachael. "Don't tell me I missed Bible study again. I thought I might make it in time today. I thought I gave myself extra time to get here to study with you ladies." He looked at Ruthie and Rachael. "What did I miss today?"

"Ach, Robert. Rachael accepted Jesus and asked Him into her heart. What a blessing to be a part of this miracle! Of course, God knew it would happen. It is always such a beautiful thing to witness when someone gives his or her life to Christ. It is too bad you were not here, but God was!" Ruthie laughed and cried at the same time. She hugged Rachael, and so did Robert.

"Remember, Rachael, Jesus will be walking right beside you, and yes, my dear, you can talk to Him as though He were standing right beside you. If someone were to hear you talking out loud, they may think you a little *wunnerlich* (strange)." Ruthie giggled at that. "However, He can hear you when you speak to Him silently. He knows everything in our hearts. Lean on Him, Rachael, and of course, you know Ruthie and I will always be here for you."

"Denki, Robert. I am so grateful for all you and Ruthie do for us. I am not sure how I feel. Being brought up to be humble and to act accordingly makes it hard for me to jump up and down, but that is exactly what I feel like doing right this minute! It is such a feeling of … cleanliness and joy. I'm feeling as though my heart is bubbling over with the love of Christ." Rachael laughed. "Yes, it is the love I feel from my heavenly Father. However, it would not have happened if not for the two of you. Thank you so much."

"It is God's work, not ours," Robert said. "And yes, it would have happened. God knew who was His before time began. Remember, Jesus said if it hadn't been Judas Iscariot who betrayed Him, it could have even been a rock. It had to be done as it was prophesied. We are just happy to be servants unto the Lord. If you feel you have much weight on your shoulders, pray to God and give it all up to Him. He takes our burdens from us. Pray for God to show you what He wants you do to for Him. Rachael, ask with a humble servant's heart and wait on the Lord. He will answer in His timing."

"To answer your questions as to what we studied," Ruthie said, "we prayed for Rachael and went over a few verses in Romans. That was just about the time you were driving up. Robert, do you mind since it is time for the children to start their studies with you that I drive Rachael home? It's much warmer now since she walked over this morning, and I won't be gone long."

"Why of course. Please honey, you don't need to ask," Robert said. He looked at his wife with that look of concern both were hiding.

Rachael hesitated, but Ruthie took her arm and led her to the car. "We will explain to Joseph that you experienced one of your spells."

"I would imagine Joseph wouldn't think that out of the ordinary since I have had quite a few of these spells of late," Rachael said.

"I'm thinking about your leaving the new Bible here. Rachael, you need to let God intervene on your behalf as far as the Bible is concerned. You need to have that Bible with you always. The comfort you will find in the pages of God's Word as times get harder for you, nothing can compare," Ruthie offered her opinion.

"Ach, maybe you are right. Joseph doesn't even want to talk to me about my illness. He always walks out when the doctors bring up anything concerning my illness. But ignoring it will not make it go away. Ruthie, would you be there when the time comes for Joseph and especially my children? I want them to all know Jesus as Lord and Savior."

"Of course, Rachael. You need not ask. We were always close growing up. With my mamm becoming Mennonite before she joined church is the only reason we were not kept from each other before we were even a thought. I am going to miss you," Ruthie said as she turned into Joseph and Rachael's lane. It was all she could do not to fall apart. Her heart was breaking, but she knew Rachael needed her to be strong for her.

"I know how much you have missed your mamm since her passing a few years ago," Rachael said softly.

"Jah, but knowing I will see her again one day does make it easier," Ruthie replied as she pulled up to where Joseph was.

When the car came to a stop, Joseph stood there with a frown on his face. He was obviously upset. As Rachael eased herself out of the car, he grabbed her arm.

"What are you doing in that car with the weather being so nice? We do not live that far from Ruthie." Joseph pulled on his wife's arm, trying to lead her away. He gave Ruthie a look of disdain.

"Joseph, please try not to act so hateful," Rachael said. She pulled away and walked to the car. She turned to Joseph and said kindly. "I walked over this morning and became ill. I do not feel well. Will you please help me to bed after I say gut-bye to Ruthie?"

Rachel addressed Ruthie. "Denki, Ruthie, for all the love you have shown me. You have been a great strength to me. Please tell Robert denki for me."

"I will," Ruthie said as she got back into her car. She didn't appreciate Joseph being so mean to her cousin. "You know you are always welcome. We love you being a part of our family, and we want to be there for you. Please let us know if you need us," Ruthie said as she started the car.

"Are you so sick you have to go to bed? What about supper and the kinner?" Joseph was glaring at her.

"The girls can put together a meal. Soup and sandwiches will be plenty for this evening. The girls can add a couple of jars of our canned vegetables. Ach Joseph, please. We must start talking and preparing."

"Stop, I don't want to hear about you not getting better! You have been going to those doctors long enough that you should be well!" Joseph was exasperated.

Rachael swayed and lost her balance. She actually felt dizzy. Joseph caught her as she tried to find her balance.

"I am scared, Rachael! I could not get along without you. I am sorry I get upset. I don't know how to deal with this except to work day and night and try not to think about it. The only way I have been able to cope is to ignore it all. Honey, are you all right?" Joseph asked, taking her arm and helping her into the house.

"No Joseph, I am not all right. Please help me upstairs. I will lie down, and then I will try to explain." Rachael pleadingly looked deep into his eyes.

Chapter 4

Laura thought back to the previous day; her party had indeed been a surprise. The only thing better than that was the thrill of seeing Jacob there. *Ach, he is so handsome, and he likes me!* Laura was too deep in thought to have heard her mamm calling her repeatedly.

"Jah, Mamm. I'm sorry I didn't hear you."

"Jah, I realize you didn't hear me. Were you daydreaming about your party? Did you enjoy yourself?" Rebeka asked.

"Ach, Mamm, I truly did." Laura was glowing.

"I noticed you were very sweet on that young Jacob. How do you know him? Where did you meet him?"

"I met him at Saturday market. I stumbled, and he caught me." Laura sighed. "And yes, Mamm, before you even ask, I was a perfect lady in his presence."

"Well, I certainly am glad to hear that, but I would expect nothing less of you. You have no idea how hard it was to keep your party a secret from you."

"But it surprised me to see so many people when we drove up," Laura said. "And Abby waiting out front to greet me. That warmed my heart. The twins with all their antics, playing with all their cousins, were fun to watch. All the adults were teasing me about starting the singings and trying to match me up with their sons or other relatives. Well, I want to enjoy my rumschpringe. I don't intend to settle down any time soon, not until the required time."

"Laura, as long as you behave as a lady should and don't let the boys take liberties, I will trust you," Rebeka said, as any Amish mother would. Rebeka thought to herself that with Laura being a little wild, she would have to keep her in prayer. Hopefully, with sweet Abby around, Laura won't be as difficult. Rebeka finished her thought as Abby walked in. Laura looked relieved to see Abby. The conversation had turned way too serious.

"Well Abby, how nice to see you. What brings you by?" Rebeka asked.

"I just came by to visit with Laura," Abby said. "That is, if Laura has her chores finished." Abby knew Laura always procrastinated about her chores.

"Ach, Mamm, may I have some time to visit with Abby?" Laura asked.

"Well of course. I hope you two have a nice time. Just don't be gone all day," Rebeka said with some concern in her voice.

Laura and Abby walked away. "Abby, you came none too soon. My mamm started lecturing me on how to behave around boys, like I don't already know. I get so tired of her nagging me," Laura said rather harshly.

"You need to be more thankful that you have a mamm who cares enough to instruct you in the way a young woman should behave," Abby replied. "Look at all the Englischer kids. So many of them are always in trouble. Do you really want to go down that path?"

"You are so judgmental of them. You just hear what our People want you to hear. They want to scare us so we won't befriend any Englischers. Our parents seem as though they don't want us to have any fun."

"Ach, Laura, don't discount our parents' wisdom. Remember, they have all been through rumschpringe, and they know the problems that can befall us during ours. Sometimes, what we deem fun can lead to *druwwel* (trouble)."

"I don't believe everything they tell us. They can't be all that bad. I am going to enjoy my rumschpringe, and that includes meeting Englischer kids. Our People all seem to want to hide from the world except for Saturday markets, when they are all too happy the Englischers come and buy their goods. They would like to keep us away from them altogether. Well, it just makes me want to explore that world all the more," Laura said rather haughtily.

"Laura, I will do everything to convince you otherwise. Nothing good can come of you exploring the Englischers' world. I will be praying for you. You are my best friend. You are like a sister to me. It would break my heart if you got into trouble or if I lost you to the world."

"You worry too much, Abby. I'll be just fine," Laura stated curtly.

"I just don't understand why you are so angry most of the time," Abby said. "Your attitude is like an angry mother bear protecting her cubs. There are those of us that love you and want the best for you. You are hard to talk to anymore. Sometimes, I feel as though I have already lost you to the world. I can't stand seeing this change in you. I didn't have to go to school those extra two years. I was afraid if I weren't there for you, you would be in druwwel, so I went."

"No one asked you to do that. I still don't see why my parents made me go. But looking back on these past two years, I realize I would not have made the Englisch friends we now know," Laura said.

"Laura, the bishop and your parents should have thought twice about your going past eighth grade. I don't think it did you any good. I see a young woman looking toward the world instead of our People. You have to see everything as if the glass is half empty. I prefer to see the glass half full. Accepting God's plan for your life would bring much joy and happiness to you. I want to please God, so whatever comes my way, I want it to be His will be done, not mine. Please think about what you are doing. You make your life so much harder than it need be. You would be so much happier if you could accept God's gift of peace and grace." Abby sighed.

"You sound like my mother, and I am sick of it. Sometimes, you get on my nerves with your Goody Two-shoes attitude. Just let me alone if all you want to do is preach to me. I'll be just fine," Laura said curtly.

Laura didn't understand how her words and actions were hurting her best friend, and Abby, being the person she was, didn't let it show. She went on as though Laura's hurtful remarks hadn't bothered her.

"All right, Laura. I just pray God watches over you. Now enough of this talk. Did you enjoy yourself at your party?"

"I did have a *wunderbaar gut* time with all my friends and family. It just tickled me pink to see Jacob there. He is so cute. Isn't it exciting? We get to start our rumschpringe soon! I can't wait. How about you?"

"I am excited," Abby said. "However, I will also guard my heart. I know that some of our youth do partake of all the liberties we are allowed, but I will not do that. I will save kissing and handholding for the man God intends me to marry."

"You can be such a prude sometimes. There is no harm in kissing and handholding," Laura said in an arrogant tone.

"We are entitled to our own opinions," Abby said softly.

"How about we walk into town for a soda?" Laura asked. She felt the need to change the subject.

"Jah. That sounds like a gut idea. Some fun should lighten the mood, don'tcha think?"

Rebeka had unintentionally overheard the girls. It hurt her heart to hear Laura being so mean to Abby. *What on earth can I do with her?* she thought. She wanted to tell Laura not to go to town, but she held her tongue.

As the girls walked along, the conversation became light; they did not bicker. The girls entered town, and it thrilled Laura as she looked around. She saw everything with new eyes. Laura felt Abby would act just like the prude she was during her rumschpringe—nothing but a wet blanket.

As they walked down the street, Laura and Abby were greeted by some Englischer kids who were about their age. At first, the girls were shy and standoffish, but Laura began to warm to the young men's charm.

Abby, however, was more cautious. She didn't want to get too close to these worldly kids. That, she thought, would lead only to *druwwel*. The Englischer kids were on their way to the Soda Shoppe and invited the girls to come along.

At first, it was just out of curiosity that the Englischer kids approached the girls, but soon thereafter, they became fast friends as they enjoyed sodas together.

Laura thought her new friends were fun and exciting, but she could tell Abby wasn't thinking along those same lines. Laura and Abby excused themselves to walk outside ahead of the others. She knew as soon as they were out of earshot of the others, Abby would let her have it.

Laura was right. She received an earful from Abby, who thought they would get into trouble by hanging out with them. Abby didn't mince any words. Though she was usually the soft-spoken one, she felt her friend needed a wake-up call. Abby felt God would not approve either.

"Ach mei, Laura! Please don't hang out with those kids. I don't trust them. Something is wrong. I can't put my finger on it, but I feel the Lord speaking to me. Did you see the complexion and teeth on that one girl? My mamm says when they look like that, they are usually on drugs. She said she read about it in a magazine at a doctor's office. And did you smell them? I think they smoke, but it is not a cigarette smell. It smelled like skunk."

"Ach, Abby. They were being so nice to us. Why do you need to be so negative? I wish you could keep your opinions to yourself about them. Don't say anything to our parents about them." Laura was stern.

Abby agreed with that, but it went against her better judgment. She agreed to go with Laura back into the Soda Shoppe. Laura told her new friends that she and Abby wanted to hang out a little while longer. Abby felt the need to watch out for Laura, so she went along begrudgingly.

Lord, please help Laura not to be influenced by those kids. We are not to judge, but we need to use good judgment, Abby prayed. She knew she needed to pray for Laura. *God, help me stay out of trouble and be a gut example for Laura and the Englischer kids.*

Abby wanted to be courted by a nice Amish boy and stay in accordance with the Old Order. She would never intentionally worry her mamm as Laura did hers. However, she wanted to remain close to her best friend. She knew Laura didn't always make good decisions. She was afraid to be with the Englischers for both of their sakes. However, she was Laura's friend and wanted to keep her safe from a world neither of them knew anything about. *As it is said, "As a man believes in his heart, so is he,"* she thought. She knew that if she didn't stay close to Laura and something happened to her that she could have prevented, she would never forgive herself.

Abby and Laura listened as the Englischers came up with a plan. Some wanted to go down to the river, and others wanted to go the mercantile store. The group decided on the store.

Laura didn't know that Larry, the leader of the group, had made plans for her and Abby. He had made a rule sometime back that anyone who wanted to hang out with his group had to undergo an initiation. He had listened to his father, Judge Bush, tell stories about what had gone on while he was in college, and the initiations he had heard about had intrigued him.

The group entered the store and walked around. Larry took Laura and Abby aside to tell them the rules. "You have to steal something from here and not get caught."

Abby and Laura were shocked that people even thought about stealing, especially from Sam, the owner. He'd always been so good to their People. Everyone knew stealing was wrong. Abby looked at Laura. "They want us to steal. I won't do it." She looked at Larry. She realized the two of them were going to butt heads. She feared for Laura, as she was a follower and would do anything to be one of them. *God, please give me the wisdom and the words to help my friend. I love Laura so much and want to keep her safe,* Abby prayed.

"Larry, I just don't feel right about doing what you are asking of us. I do want to be friends with all of you, but we are taught that stealing is wrong," Laura said softly. She wanted him to like her.

"Ah Laura, it's no big deal. It's not like they'll even notice anything missing or that you were the one who took it," Larry said with a smirk.

"But I will know, and so will God. I can't do it," Laura said.

"Okay. We'll drop it for now."

"Ach, thank you, Larry," Laura said sweetly.

"Laura, we need to head home. It is getting late. Our mamms will be expecting us soon," Abby urged.

"Yes, you are right," Laura said. She turned to the others. "Well, I will see you all later. It was nice meeting all of you." Laura bid her new friends good-bye. She gave Larry a bit of a grin. She lowered her head. She and Abby started home.

"They were so nice, and what fun! It will be so exciting when we start going to the singings, or say we are, so we can come to town and hang out with them. I liked Larry, J.C., Ashley, and the rest of them, didn't you?" Laura asked.

"Laura, how can you say they were nice? They wanted us to steal from Sam! I will not change my mind about stealing or about them. You have no business being friends with them."

"No one says you have to hang out with us," Laura stated.

"What? And leave you alone with those wild, disrespectful Englischers? I wouldn't do that. I don't have any peace about them," Abby said.

"I don't think they are that bad. I bet they wouldn't have let us go through with actually taking the items," Laura said, trying to defend her new friends.

"Ach, Laura, you are so naïve. You don't believe that, do you? Please be careful. You want to take part in the Englischers' world so bad you would let yourself believe anything. I love you and don't want to see you get hurt."

"You are like a sister to me. I respect your opinion most of the time, but you are wrong about my new friends. I believe you are jealous," Laura said. She started walking faster; she wanted to end the conversation.

"I can see there is no talking to you, Laura, so let's just drop the subject once again as we did earlier to keep from arguing," Abby said in a sad tone.

Their trek home became uncomfortably silent. The two girls had never had harsh words with each other, Laura thought, and that bothered her. But she decided that was not sufficient reason to stay away from her new friends. She wanted to get home, be by herself, and think about Larry. She could not believe Abby would act so self-righteously. *How dare she?* Laura thought.

Abby was shocked that Laura thought the Englischers were nice. She shook her head and looked to her Father in heaven for help.

When they reached Abby's house, Laura said good-bye and kept walking. Abby said good-bye, turned and went up the lane to her house.

Abby greeted her mamm and went about her chores. Her mamm noticed that Abby looked sad. The smile that always crossed Abby's face was not there. Martha couldn't remember seeing her sweet daughter so distraught, but she decided not to ask her about it. She figured that when Abby was ready to talk, she would seek her guidance. Martha needed to go to the barn. She called out to Abby to let her know she would be right back.

After Martha walked out, Abby took advantage of the empty house to pray. *God, please give me strength to get through to Laura before she makes a big mistake.* She began muttering to herself, and she became so engrossed in her thoughts that she didn't hear her mamm return.

Martha didn't mean to overhear her daughter as she walked in, but the house was so quiet that she heard every word. She couldn't remember her daughter being this upset with Laura ever. But she wasn't going to pry; she left Abby to her thoughts and prayers. She didn't want to make a big deal about Abby being gone all day. She would give her space to make mistakes, to learn from them, as Abby's mistakes had always been so minor.

Laura ran all the way home from Abby's house so she would be home on time for her chores. She rushed into the house and began working at once.

Her mamm heard Laura come in and noticed she was out of breath. She assumed Laura must have run all the way from Abby's house. As she hugged her daughter, Rebeka noticed a funny smell coming from Laura. *Could that be cigarettes?* "Laura, you sure were in a hurry. Did you not give yourself enough time to get home? You have a funny smell on your clothing. Where have you and Abby been?"

"We met some new friends today, mamm."

"That's nice, but that doesn't explain the smell on you." Rebeka raised her eyebrows.

"Mamm I promise, I didn't smoke. The smell is from some of the kids who smoke."

"Ach, Laura, I hope we are not going to have to worry about you during your running-around time. Tell me some of the things you did today. What are your new friends like?" Rebeka questioned.

"Abby and I walked into town, and that is when we met them. They seemed very interesting. They like hanging out at the Soda Shoppe and wandering in and out of other stores afterwards," Laura explained. She sure couldn't tell her mamm they wanted Abby and her to steal something to join their group. "They all go to the Englischer high school, and like I told you, they smoke."

"Laura, are you sure you want to be friends with Englischer kids? Why would they want to be wandering the stores if they are not in there to buy something? You just don't understand the druwwel you can get into with worldly kids. There are so many things you have no experience with. I am concerned for you."

Rebeka, remembering her own running-around period, shook her head. She didn't want her daughter to go through what she had gone through that broke her heart, which still hurt from what had happened during her rumschpringe. The memories were buried deep in her heart and soul; they had never gone away. She still woke some nights in a deep sweat from nightmares. She shuddered thinking about what had transpired.

"Mamm, you can't keep me from experiencing my rumschpringe." Laura tensed up. She stood tall, looking her mamm eye to eye. "Our rules say you must allow me to have the freedom to explore the Englischer world without your influence."

"Jah, that is true to a point. We have rules in this house that you must follow. We will abide by your rumschpringe as long as you respect us and our rule." Rebeka met her daughter's look, eye to eye. She would not be talked down to by her daughter or by anyone else for that matter.

∞

Chapter 5

Rachael felt so safe in Joseph's strong arms. He had always been such a gut husband and daed. How could she make him understand about the cancer let alone her having accepted Jesus as her Lord and Savior without him hitting the roof? She and the doctors had tried to talk to him many times. However, today it all had to come out no matter how upset he got.

She prayed fervently. *Please God, help me plant that mustard seed, and please Father, water it and make it grow! Jesus is the way, the truth, and the life to our salvation. Please soften my Joseph's heart so he will see just how wonderful it is to have Your Son in his life. Lord, please give me the wisdom and the right words to explain. Thank You, Father, in Your Son's most precious name, Amen.*

In the mere seconds it took Rachael to pray, the Holy Spirit filled her with the peace she desperately needed. She seemed to feel stronger, if not in body, in spirit for sure and for certain.

Joseph helped Rachel up the stairs and into their room. He gently laid her on their bed and put his pillow behind her head. "Are you comfortable?"

"Jah I am as comfortable as we can make it. Denki, Joseph. I think it is about time for Marty to be home from school. They can fix the soup and sandwiches. It will not throw either of them into a dither. Ach, Joseph, they are such gut kinner, all of them. Just let them know you and I need some time alone to talk and to let us know when dinner is on the table."

Joseph descended the stairs; he saw that the girls were already in the kitchen checking the pies in the oven. Allie looked up and smiled at her daed, but her smile quickly faded. "Daed, what is wrong?" Marty came over and clung to Allie's arm; she also wanted to hear what her daed had to say.

Joseph reached for his girls and pulled them into a loving embrace. "It is fine. Your mamm asked you girls to prepare dinner and of course to do your regular chores."

Marty gave him a squeeze that told him of her love. "Allie and I can fix dinner, Daed, so don't worry."

"Your mamm and I need to talk. Would you run out to the barn and let your brooders know I will be busy?" Joseph asked Allie.

As Mammi Ingersoll, Rachel's mother, entered the room, she asked the girls, "How is your mamm doing?"

"What do you mean, Mammi?" Marty asked. That gave Allie just enough time to look at her mammi and with pleading eyes, shook her head as if to say, *Please don't ask anything more.*

Mammi smiled. She understood Allie. "Well, let's just say your mamm is very wise and her love for the Lord and her family is testimony to that."

Allie finished putting biscuits into a pan as Marty announced the apple pies were done. "What gut timing, Marty," Allie said smiling. She helped her sister take them out of the oven. "These pies are beautiful, sister. Mamm did teach you well. Your pies are exceptional!"

Allie let Mammi and Marty know she wouldn't be gone long. She shot out to the barn to do her father's bidding. She announced to her brooders that her father needed to spend time speaking with their mamm. After delivering the message, her long legs carried her back to the house.

Allie and Marty were teasing each other, which brought joy to Mammi's heart. Marty had tried to follow in Allie's footsteps for as long as Mammi could remember. She had from the time she had started walking. She loved her big sister and wanted to be just like her.

One thing Rachael had always done in the privacy of their home is to tease and play with her kinner and family. She knew each moment of life was precious. She wanted her family to enjoy life and thought it too short not to have fun. She wanted to act properly, as the bishop expected, but she wanted her home to be filled with fun and laughter. Their playful bouts around the house brought a smile to her each time she thought about it.

Joseph was upstairs with his beloved wife, who gave him for the past several hours some insight into her condition. Now he realized he had only gleaned a glimpse of her condition thus far. He sat quietly pondering the many issues that hung heavily on Rachael's heart.

Rachael started with a prayer after asking Joseph to allow it, not a silent one, but one where she just talked to God out loud as if she knew Him personally.

As Joseph listened he heard her asked God to soften his heart. *Does she think my heart not gentle? Well, our bishop will not put up with this. What can I do?* He then heard Rachael ask God to give her the strength she would need to help her family come to Christ. *That will not sit well with* Bishop *Malachi Strapp either.* He couldn't fathom what they would be up against.

As she finished her prayer, Joseph became deadly silent. *Mad* did not begin to express the feelings running through his mind. The Lapp family, all Old Order Amish, had never stepped foot into another church as far back as Joseph could remember. *Jesus, Lord and Savior? Was Jesus her best friend? She wants me to trust in Jesus as my Lord of Lords! Has she lost her ever loving mind? Rachael knew darn well it wasn't in their beliefs. What arrogance! We know Jesus is God's Son, but we are to pray to God. Where has she gotten this information she is spewing?, She is just being haughty!*

Joseph felt he must have worn holes in the big, braided rugs Rachael had made the first couple years of their marriage as he paced back and forth. But it didn't diminish the wrath he kept under his hat just under the boiling point. *We go to church, we believe in God, and we do good works in helping our neighbors. Standing before God on Judgment Day is when we find out if what we have done deems us worthy enough to enter into heaven,* Joseph told himself.

He thought, however, that he heard someone speaking to his heart. He shook his head to clear it of the thought. The voice was saying, "*Lean on Me, have faith.*" Shaking his head, he wondered where the words had come from. He questioned his sanity.

Joseph looked at his beautiful but ever so frail wife. How could he stay upset with her? Well, he thought, he would hear her out and ask that she keep all this Jesus stuff in the privacy of their bedroom.

Rachael smiled weakly and patted the side of the bed, encouraging him to sit with her. Joseph sat next to her, his shoulders slumped with sadness.

Rachael knew she must forge ahead with everything. Joseph needed to know all about her cancer and that the doctors hadn't given her much time to put her affairs in order. She began slowly telling him about the cancer and that the treatments weren't working.

Joseph admitted he didn't want to hear what she needed to tell him. He told her he felt sorry for walking out of the doctor's office when they were speaking of the cancer and the treatments. Joseph also admitted he didn't want to hear how sick the cancer made her. He realized how wrong he had been. The cancer was winning. He was losing.

"Joseph, please look at me. Let God help us through this time. Draw strength from God. He will be there for us if you just let Him. I accepted what God dealt me. Instead of getting mad, I chose to give my heart to Jesus, asking Him to come live there. I've asked forgiveness of my sins and can't tell you how light my heart feels. Joseph, my love, I am not afraid to die. I want you to understand I read enough of the Bible to know I needed Jesus to enter heaven. Please try to understand. I didn't read more of the Bible to go against you," Rachael pleaded.

"Where did you get this new Bible?" Joseph asked.

"Ruthie gave it to me, but it was my decision to read it. Jesus tells us, 'None come to the Father except through Me.' After reading the Gospel of John, I made up my own mind I wanted eternity," Rachael confessed.

Joseph held Rachael's frail hand; tears ran down his face. How were they going to keep this a secret so they didn't come under the *Bann*?

Rachael reached up wiping Joseph's tear stained face. She knew he couldn't deal with all this unless he accepted Jesus into his heart.

Oh God, what can we do? Joseph asked the Lord. *Here, my wife is so sick, and I have not taken her needs seriously. I have been neglecting her in her time of need. Please open my ears and my heart to her needs. Please forgive me, Father.* When Joseph looked up, he saw Rachael watching and waiting on him.

"Joseph, please let us show our children the love of Christ through us. We need to be strong and united in our salvation through Christ. Will you do this for me? My doctors are telling me my time is short. I need you to be strong for us; God can be your strength through this if you let Him." Rachael pleaded.

"What did the doctors say again? Shutting you out every time you brought them up did not help you. We should have been dealing with this together. Rachael, I am so sorry, my love. Please forgive me. I am so scared, my *liewi*. Obviously my faith isn't as strong as yours. I should have been the husband you needed, one you could have leaned on. Instead, you have had to carrying this burden alone. Please, Rachael, forgive me for being so selfish, being so locked inside myself. I've been a horrible husband." Joseph's tears flowed like small rivers down his weather worn face.

"Joseph, there is nothing to forgive, and you are not a horrible husband. You have been the best husband and daed to our kinner any woman could have ever asked for. I would like for you to come to my next doctor's appointment with me. Will you?"

"Yes, my liewi, but tell me again what you know about your illness. I need a little time to digest this."

"Well, it is some kind of cancer. Mine started in my stomach, and then it traveled up to my lungs and lymph nodes. That is why I lost so much weight. It makes it hard to eat. The medications they gave me aren't helping, and they make me so nauseated. They asked me if I wanted to go for chemotherapy months ago, but I declined. The doctor told me with the cancer being this far advanced, we would have to use the medicine aggressively, but there is no hope. That is why I declined. God gave me a peace about letting go. He is my Father, and He has an appointed time for each of His children to come home. My time is near."

"It is so hard for me to hear this. As for our talking about Christ, I feel we need to keep it in our own home as we for sure and for certain will be placed under the Bann, and at this time, we need all our family to be near us. So this discussion needs to stay between us and our immediate house," Joseph said.

"I agree with you, at least for now," Rachael said. "Joseph, will you please study the complete New Testament with me so you might learn where my peace comes from?"

"Rachael, are you positive this new Bible is what we should study?" Joseph raised his voice as he looked at her frail body.

"Ach mei! My dear Joseph, this is not what we should be focusing on. My end is very near, and the doctors want me to get all my affairs in order, as does Ruthie. I continued to go several times a week to her house long after I became ill. Ruthie continued to pay me, but she would not let me lift a finger at her place because she knew how sick I was and that we needed the money."

"So if you weren't working, what were you doing?" Joseph asked. He had started pacing again. Someone was speaking to him again. *"Lean on Me. Have faith."* He realized it was truly God speaking to him. He bent his head in shame. His wife had found such peace in the Bible; he decided to do as she asked. It couldn't hurt him to look at this Bible in his bedroom with his wife. "Yes dear, I will study the New Testament with you," Joseph said with a bent head and a humbled heart.

Rachael sat watching, letting Joseph work through his anger and frustration and saw him coming back to his sweet self. *God is so good*, she thought. *He is working on my husband's heart this minute. Thank You, Lord.*

Joseph looked at his wife, who was smiling sweetly. "Oh my sweet wife, how have you put up with me all these years? I am always ranting about something, especially here lately. I can't begin to tell you how much I love you. You are the light of my life. How will I ever make it here without you? What do you need me to do to make things easier on you? Is there any pain? Do you want a tray brought up?" Joseph asked with a breaking heart.

"Ach mei, no!" Rachael laughed. "Let's go on with our lives as normally as possible for as long as we can. We need to talk more before we tell the rest of the family how advanced the cancer is." She could tell just how hard this was for him; the pain and the tears in his eyes were obvious. "We can't wait many more days. I am asking that the two of us spend time praying and seeking God. You are the head of this family and should be the one to explain it to the children."

"What do you say we go down to dinner when you are ready?" Joseph asked. He squeezed her hand.

"Don't you want to know a little more about the cancer and what we all are to expect as the days go by?" she asked.

"Yes, I guess I do need to know more, don't I? The kids are going to ask many questions. They will have such a hard time with all of this, and so will your parents."

"My mamm knows some. She helped me in so many ways. Not only with household chores, but also with strengthening my walk with Christ. She devoted herself to our church, but she read on her own the whole Bible. So she knew I needed Christ to have eternal life and to be waiting for all my family up there. My immediate family at least, which is my utmost prayer."

"You mean to say that Mamm has accepted Jesus? What makes you all believe that Jesus is Lord and Savior?"

"Reading John 3:16 is what did it for me. When we can sit with a Bible and study, I will show you several verses that touched my heart. However, John 3:16 reached right out there and grabbed me. As for my mamm, she kept it to herself as she did not want to influence anyone else for fear of it getting back to the brethren. But yes, she believes Jesus is her Lord and Savior."

"I need some time with all this salvation stuff. And with all the years of our doctrine, I am going to ask God to speak to me. I will ask for God's will to be done for us," Joseph said. He smiled at Rachael.

"I saw you turn your head sideways and up a few minutes ago. Did you hear the kids or something outside?" Rachael asked.

"Funny you should ask that. After you shared Christ with me and I was having doubts, it was as though someone whispered, 'Lean on Me. Have faith.'"

"Ach mei! That is the Holy Spirit speaking to your heart. Satan can put thoughts into our minds, but he can't read our thoughts as God can.

However, Satan would not put good thoughts in our minds, especially about God!"

They were together in their room for several hours. Joseph was realizing how much he had missed by not going with Rachael to her doctor appointments. He was listening for the first time.

"Joseph, God gave me a wonderful feeling of peace. Give it a chance, will ya? Now let me tell you about my condition. My medications will have to be increased soon as the pain worsens."

"I should already know all of this." Joseph shook his head.

"I will continue to lose weight. It will get to the point I won't be able to eat much, and toward the end, probably not at all. I sure do not expect the family to eat differently. This household will run as normally as possible, as we said before. It will make it easier for me to visit and enjoy my family if we fix a small sofa close to the kitchen. I want to be right in the middle of my family for as long as I can. I want to make things as fun and light as possible. Please help me make this a happy time with lots of gut memories." Rachael gave Joseph's hand a pat.

"Well, my dear wife, it sounds as though you have figured everything out, and it is what will happen. Anything we can do we will. I do believe your praying before we started gave me the strength and desire to listen. It is hard for me to think about my life without you. I've loved you from the moment I laid eyes on you. As I remember it, you played hard to get. I believe that made me love you all the more. My girl had spunk! What did it take, five months before you finally accepted my invitation to ride home in my courting buggy? That was one of the highlights of my life. The many special things and the memories you created are just too many to count," Joseph said lovingly. He was trying to regroup before he broke down. He knew his wife didn't need to be worrying about him or his feelings. It should be all about her, not him. "When do you want to talk to the children about your illness?" Joseph asked.

"My dear, you know the children as well as I do. However, with the boys working with you, it made you closer to them as the girls are with me. I am thinking that the boys will be able to respond to you better. However, knowing Allie as I do, the boys have probably been given a heads-up. They will be more aware than Marty. Marty is the only one who doesn't know anything. I know my mamm has shared some with my daed. What a blessing from God that Mammi's health has remained so good. Her mind is still sharp as a tack, and she can be there to help you. With the two girls to help, she should be fine for a good many years. Again, let us praise God!"

"After dinner, we will have our family meeting. I would like to start a new tradition before we eat. I would like it if you would say grace for us. It won't take me long to feel confident enough to take over our prayers at meals and family devotions. Where would you start in the New Testament? Should I read from the beginning?" Joseph asked.

"Oh, Joseph what a wunderbaar gut idea! I believe the Gospel of John is where I would like you to start. It tells about Jesus' love for us. He came as God in the flesh. The first of this gospel tells of John the Baptist, who came to baptize of water before Jesus arrived, telling the people to repent and be baptized. The Gospel of John is written by one of Jesus' apostles who was is referred to as the one He loved. Does that make sense to you, my liewi?"

"Jah. It is a little confusing, but with your help and this Word, I believe I can come to understand it as you do." Joseph reached over and in one swoop picked Rachael up. She put her arm around his neck and leaned her head on his shoulder. As they entered the hallway just out from the kitchen, Joseph gently lowered her to her feet. He extended his arm, and she gladly took hold to steady herself. She gave him a reassuring pat as they entered the kitchen.

"Daed, Mamm, we were just going to send out a dinner call," Allie said.

"What is this feast on the table? Did you cook all this, Mammi? It smells wunderbaar gut. I believe I can eat my share for sure and for certain," Rachael said with tears in her eyes. *God is so good*, she thought.

"Family, let us sit down to this meal and enjoy it. After eating the dessert Marty fixed, we will sit around the table for a while," Joseph said as he took his place at the head of the table.

Rachael looked up to see if Joseph wanted to say grace. He shook his head no. He said, "Next time, I promise." The family bowed their heads for the silent prayer. Rachael knew that Joseph was good for his word and that the next meal would be said with a prayer to God the Father. Rachael sighed as she bowed her head. *God is so good.*

∞

Chapter 6

Micah felt blessed spending another beautiful night with Mary, well into the wee hours anyway. The evenings he spent in the buggy riding alongside Mary and talking of their future always flew by. He never tired of her company.

The longer they were together, the more he wanted to kiss her. He could look into her eyes and see the same yearning. They knew they must be careful to stay pure in heart and mind. When moments seemed tense, Mary would change the subject and the conversation would lighten. She was always able to turn some small thing into laughter for them. He felt very grateful for that. He wanted to treat her respectfully, and with his family upbringing and their faith, he knew that was what God expected of him.

Since they were both nineteen, they planned to speak to their families, go through instruction and baptism, and be published at the same time. Being published is what takes place after the couple go through instruction, get baptized and then the bishop publishes the couple. In essence, the bishop announces the date of the wedding as the Old Order Amish have a wedding season. It is also after the celery is matured and cut. They both were very mature, and Micah felt he could support a wife.

His woodworking, especially his roll top desks, were in high demand. Micah had apprenticed to his Uncle Robert for the past several years. His uncle had a shop in town with lots of furniture on display for the Englischers, and he did quite well.

Micah's Uncle Robert being more than fair with him allowed Micah to put away quite a sum of money into his nest egg. He had made Mary some special pieces, starting with a larger hope chest he gave her for Christmas the previous year.

Mary's daed was a good farmer and carpenter in most circumstances, but he didn't like working with the smaller tools one must use for any special carvings, whereas Micah loved etching designs into each piece of furniture he created.

Micah talked to Mary's brother before making the hope chest. He wanted Abraham to be pleased for Mary receiving such a beautiful piece of furniture. Micah prayed Abraham wouldn't see it as too fancy. Mary would need to start her own home someday and needed a place to store the items she made for their home. He had many other furniture items tucked away for later.

As a general rule the Amish homes were sparsely furnished and decorated. Being a carpenter, Micah wanted Mary to have all she needed. Of course, the customers would come first. He and his Uncle Robert worked well together and his uncle had taught him how to work the different designs into the wood to be pleasing to the eye of the Englischers. Their Englischer customers spent more money on their furnishings, adding even more to Micah's egg nest. Some of the Mennonites bought a little more extravagantly. They even had automobiles and used electricity, so why not fancy furniture?

Each piece Robert Miller made was a work of art. Not one flaw anywhere. He took extra pains to do the very best job he could in creating each masterpiece. Micah was proud of his uncle's work.

Uncle Robert was a loving man toward his family and a man of God. He loved everyone, including Micah and Jacob. He and his family lived by the Word of God. *'As for me and my house we shall serve the Lord.'* This carved plaque hung above the kitchen door to remind them. Uncle Robert always gave the credit for his work to God. There was always a happiness about him that radiated God's grace and peace.

Micah's thoughts about visiting Mary that evening kept his energy flowing throughout the day. That and the strength the Lord gave him. *What a wonderful wife Mary will make*, he thought. He loved her so, but he kept his thoughts pure toward her. He would never take advantage of her. He wanted their union before God to be what God expected of them.

Micah sanding on his latest project looked up to see Jacob coming through the door; Jacob had just finished running the errands for the shop. "Hullo, Jacob. Did you get everything Uncle Robert asked for?"

"Jah, I did." Jacob sighed.

"Micah, do you think Laura would let me court her?"

"Ach mei! You have it bad for her." Micah chuckled. "You are both very young. Take it slow. That is the best advice I can give you at this time."

"Jah, you are right. It is just hard to wait. I know I have only been here a short time, but at her place the day of her birthday, every time I looked her way, I caught her looking at me. Made me believe she might be interested."

"Well cousin, be careful not to get into a rush. Her daed will be all over you like bees protecting their queen and the honey. He watched over Mary at that age too, and he's very protective, I might add. Her brother escorted her to the singings. She never gave a look in my direction for several singings. I caught her sitting on a bale of hay and surprised her by sitting down next to her. I just wanted her attention. After the first three singings in the barn we all attended, her brother and I became friends. After getting to know me a little better helped to encourage her some." Micah beamed remembering Mary's response.

"What did her brother do?" Jacob asked.

"He talked to Mary and told her he thought I would meet with their daed's approval. I thanked him. I was ever so grateful. When I first saw Mary, I knew she would be the only one for me. Her brother gave me a stern talking to, and being close to Mary, he is also very protective. He advised me not to even try to hold her hand for a time. He warned that Mary was shy and would not tolerate me stepping out of line. I had to promise to be the perfect gentleman before her brother would allow her to ride home with me," Micah shared with Jacob.

"Uncle had an old courting buggy in the back of the barn. The buggy was there when he bought the place. Even with the protection of the barn, the buggy still needed lots of work to redd it up for courting. That took time, but Uncle Robert helped me when he could spare a moment. Not much did he help, mind you, but I think he thought I needed something to keep myself busy. I just liked his company anytime he could give it.

"My suggestion, Jacob, is to buy an old buggy to reststore. That way it will take your mind off Laura. You might work off the cost by doing odd jobs for the owner. Most of the gentlemen have a soft spot for a young man getting his first courting buggy. They show a little twinkle in their eyes, remembering all those years back to their own courting days." Micah's thoughts took him back to that period in his own life.

"I do appreciate your advice. This is all so new to me," Jacob said.

"Working on a buggy will keep you busy when you are not working. That way, the time passes faster. Besides, idle hands are the devil's workshop!" Micah offered.

"But for right now, Jacob, put the items you brought back for Uncle Robert away and spindle the receipts. Then you can help me," Micah stated.

Jacob's eyes sparkled sky blue, with a smile that could light up a room; he nodded and charged off to do as he had been told. He was happy to be there. There were not many in his family who wanted to do anything but till the land. Not Jacob; he took after his uncle and cousin. He loved working with wood. Running his hand over a table top just sanded and wiped clean gave him a feeling of calmness. He noticed that he had developed muscles due to his woodworking. His arms and neck and back hurt like he had been beat up when he had first started working, but as the days went by, the pain eased and new muscles were showing themselves.

He had worked hard on the land in Ohio with his family and thought himself in good physical shape, but woodworking involved different muscles of which he felt every one of them. Uncle Robert and Micah had teased him about being out of shape, but knowing they were teasing in fun, he took it well. They finally admitted they each had the same soreness when they first started doing larger pieces. The hand sanding on larger items caused more than just a little pain until his muscles were built up.

Jacob had a hard time convincing his family to let him go to Lancaster County at age seventeen. His daed had not been nearly as against it as his mamm had been. She had kept saying, "It will be just like Micah. He was to learn the trade under his uncle and then come home. Then he met Mary not long after he arrived and lost any desire to return to home." His mamm, Iva, heartbroken over the whole ordeal, would not put it to rest.

Jacob had kept in close contact with his mamm to let her know he loved her. However, he would not be mentioning Laura to her. *Anyway, who knows?* he thought. *It might not work out for us.* His dream of courting Laura was just that, still in the dream stages.

"Micah, is that roll top desk you are working on your first?" Jacob asked.

"Jah. I waited two years before Uncle Robert thought I would be ready to tackle these big, intricate pieces of furniture. He said he wanted only twenty-five percent of what I made on my work sold out of here. I always help him with the orders that come in first. Then when things are caught up, I work on pieces for myself. I buy wood or pay for some that comes to the shop. Uncle Robert is always more than fair. He says God was good to him, so he can afford to help me get started.

"I love living with this family. Getting up in the morning, going downstairs, and joining in with the bantering is such a joy. We didn't have that at home. We all loved each other in our family, don't get me wrong. It is just not the same kind of love that permeates the air like here." Micah sat for a moment smiling; his happiness showed on his face.

"How long did you work under Uncle Robert before he started taking a percentage on your pieces of furniture?" Jacob asked.

"Well, I didn't think much about it. My thoughts were on learning from one of the best in the country," Micah answered. "I knew from when I was little that I wanted to work with wood. I remember carving small toys. Once, I made a rifle out of some oak my daed had lying around. Then a wagon came into the works. I sanded for hours until it was smooth. The feel of sanded wood is so soothing to me. Uncle, who was living in Ohio at that time, showed an interest in my woodworking abilities. He said I showed promise. My face lit up that day like the sun. Don't believe you could have wiped that smile off my face!

"So I knew from childhood I liked working with wood. You have helped on the farm, tilling, planting, and harvesting. If that felt like drudgery to you, maybe woodworking runs in your veins as it did mine," Micah said.

"As far as the percentage you ask about; it starts with the first piece. We have all the tools we need to make anything, including wood carving sets. I don't believe you should squabble over anything when uncle starts taking your twenty-five percent out."

"Thanks for our talk. I believe it helped me make my decision. I will be praying about it. Thanks again, Micah." Jacob smiled.

"You are very welcome, and remember what I said about Laura. Give it time to grow. You are both very young, especially Laura. She just turned sixteen. Make the most of your rumschpringe. It can be lots of fun no matter which girl you end up courting as long as you remember to treat her as the lady she is," Micah said. "I am still learning myself. So I can't give you much more advice, but I would like to be your friend. Even though we are cousins, we didn't get to know each other well back home. If you need anything, don't hesitate to come find me. I better start paying attention to what I am working on. Uncle Robert will be back here from his last delivery soon. He likes to see that production didn't stop while he was gone. Better get to work, both of us."

Jacob finished putting away the supplies he had purchased for the shop. Everything in its place and a place for everything, neat and tidy as his uncle was. That made it very easy to find whatever was needed in the blink of an eye.

At the Miller home, the women took gut care of their home and gardens. The barn and sheds there were kept by the two boys, but not like the woodworking shop. Uncle always wanted his customers to be able to go to the back room and watch the furniture being made. Using all hand tools seems to make a big difference in the sales. The

Englischers always liked watching their purchases come to life. Jacob turned to his project as Uncle Robert came through the back door.

"Well lads, it is gut to see you hard at work," Uncle Robert stated as he came closer to see Micah's work on the desk. "Ach, Micah, what a wunderbaar gut job on that desk. You will be outselling me soon." Robert patted Micah on the shoulder and gave him a warm smile.

There it was again, that joy Uncle Robert always carried with his presences. One day soon, Micah decided he needed to have a heart-to-heart talk with him. He wanted to know about the joy Uncle Robert carried everywhere he went.

"Thank you. Uncle Robert, how many hours do you think it takes you to make a desk like this?" Micah asked.

"That, my boy, is not anything I have ever dwelt on. When the desk is finished, it is done. God tells us not to worry or have fear. If you worry, you bring fear close to you. Every day, give your heartfelt thanks to God and pray that His will be done. When you turn all your cares over to the Lord, your work becomes easier. Never forget that. It is not to say we don't have our share of problems, but it makes them easier to bear. We also give thanks to God for things that have brought us to task. This keeps us close to God. He tells us to pray without ceasing." Robert smiled.

"Ach, just a few words from you and I feel such peace," Micah said.

"It is not me, Micah, it is God. Man may disappoint you, but God never will. Let's get to work here, boys!" Uncle Robert laughed as he joined Micah and Jacob.

The rest of the day passed quickly. When they all walked outside and closed up shop for the day, they scattered in different directions. Each had a few errands to run before heading to the Miller home for supper.

∞

Chapter 7

The Miller home was a small version of what most Amish families in that area lived in. There was a milk cow, chickens, a yearling steer almost ready for butchering, and a good-sized garden the women manicured. The house being two stories looked like it had come straight out of a magazine.

In the fall, they put up all the provisions from the garden they would need. It seemed to always carry them through to the next harvest. There were a few fruit trees and a fence on one end that held a variety of berry vines and a grape arbor. The berries and the grapes provided them with plenty for jams, jellies, and juice.

Their house held more pieces of furniture than it needed. Robert had kept telling his young wife at the beginning of their years together that he couldn't find room in the shop for this piece or that piece and would she mind having them in the house for a while. Her eyes would twinkle. She could always tell that was his way of giving her beautiful furniture. She was grateful God had given her such a gut husband. They both felt blessed with all God provided for them.

"Hello, honey." Robert gave Lisa a hug and a kiss on the cheek. "How is dinner coming? We won't be long getting our chores done, and I am sure all of the boys are starving. I know Micah and Jacob are and with all the work Thomas and Ethan have done today they are too. Thomas and Ethan did a good job repairing that barn. It had some pretty bad leaks."

"Dinner is almost ready. How are Micah and Jacob doing with you at the shop?"

"Micah is doing a wunderbaar gut job. I am so glad Elmer let him come. Micah's got the gift for woodworking in his heart. Jacob is starting to settle into a good routine in the shop. He also shows a lot of promise."

"I'm glad to have Micah here with us. He has become another son to me. I am sure Iva would not want to share that thought with me. But you were right about him. He is a thoughtful person and a gut worker. He will make a gut husband one day. Your walk with Christ is showing Micah what a true man of God is all about. By watching you, he has come a long way these past several years. Micah's mannerisms have changed. He is softer in spirit, and his smiles come easy now as though they are real. I used to think to myself that those first smiles he showed were shallow in meaning, just to pacify our feelings, as though we would not see right through that," Lisa stated smiling.

"Well, Mrs. Miller, you seem to be the observant one, ya? I do agree with you, though. I have always loved him as one of our own. His daed thinks he is doing just what God intended for him to do. He is very pleased with Micah. I wrote to let them know how gut Micah is with his hands and the wood. He really looks at the wood. Sometimes, he comes up with special designs," Robert said.

"I worry about how upset his mamm is over him wanting to stay with us in Lancaster, County. At first, some of our letters told me she felt we were trying to steal her son. I guess being her firstborn, Micah was harder to let go of. I do know he kept in contact with his family a couple times a week. He missed them also. But after meeting Mary, even though it took a little bit of time for Micah to get her attention, he was head over heels in love with her. I felt proud of Mary for making him wait. Remember that buggy he restored? That gave him plenty to keep busy with when he wasn't working with you," Lisa said, chuckling.

"We stepped back and let him do that project almost all on his own. We hadn't even thought about the horse, thinking it would take him longer to complete the buggy. Then on that Saturday, he came to you and asked if you had the time to look at a horse he found. He was so cute. He wanted his Uncle Robert's advice. I remember him telling you he thought the horse sound with gut conformation and a beautiful bay." Lisa laughed.

"I was very impressed with the conformation of the horse. He had a nice, thick breast. That gives the horse gut endurance. The bay was gentle, not at all flighty. That is important when looking for a good buggy horse. Micah obviously visited the horse many times, as the horse nestled his head up against Micah, showing its affection. I thought it a gut match right from the start. The bay was five years old and had lots more years of services ahead of him.

"Mr. Rowe's stock has always been good. He had lots of repairs for Micah to work off the cost of the bay. Elmer taught him how to work with the animals and other farming skills. But it is the woodworking that runs in Micah's blood. As far back as I can remember, instead of fishing or playing ball with the other boys, he had a knife in one hand and a piece of wood in the other. If he wasn't working on one project, he readied himself for a next one," Robert said, smiling at his memories.

"I am happy to see Micah and Mary doing some planning for the future. Micah sometimes stares off into space when he thinks no one is watching, and that smile that comes over his face makes me remember when we were courting, my dear wife," Robert said as he looked at Lisa with much love.

"Ach, Robert, you are still so romantic. That keeps me feeling young. That may be why I am almost jumping up and down with news to share with you. I'm pregnant!" Lisa said, smiling. "And twins at that."

"Ach mei! What wunderbaar gut news this is!" he said as he picked her up and swung her around. "You are still as tiny as the day I met you." They were laughing and shedding tears of joy.

"Well, I think we could certainly use a few more bobbeli around here. With the other three kids being older, it will be a joy to hear the pitter-patter of little feet again," Lisa said as she hugged her husband.

Lisa knew Paula would be happy about the news of the upcoming births, and she thought it would be good practice for Paula to be involved with the birth and care of the newborns. There were still lots of things to get done for the upcoming wedding. As a matter of fact, a tradition in the Old Order Amish is to have lots of celery for weddings and this year the celery was growing rapidly.

Their niece had been with them two years, and Lisa couldn't be happier than to help plan a wedding for Paula. The quilting bee coming up was for her. Even though she was not Paula's mother, she felt extremely close to her.

God had been so good to all of them. The extra three they had acquired in the last several years had given Lisa a yearning for even more bobbeli after the birth of her two buns in the oven. Her smile warmed her clear through.

∞

Chapter 8

Rebeka, Mary, and Laura arrived at Ellie's early for the quilting bee. Rebeka always showed up early for the women's gatherings, from canning in the fall to all the frolics. Her mamm had always done the same, saying, "There are never enough hands helping to put the lunch together and the many snacks the ladies will bring." They always worked so diligently with each other, and every stitch on every quilt had to be perfect. They would get to talking, teasing, and having fun in general, and the time would fly by. It made the frolic a light affair.

"Rebeka, how gut of you and your girls to come early to help. You have always been a good example for the rest of us. I wish more would take notice of your thoughtfulness. My girls are helpful to me, however, when we have all the extras in the house, my towheads feel the need to show off. When they were in their terrible twos, they did run us ragged, but now that they are four, it is better. They are quite the handful. ; however, my Barbie is a real lifesaver when it comes to them. She is so gut to them, and they do seem to listen to her better than most," Ellie said humbly.

"Ellie, Martha and I were just saying last Sunday how we were looking forward to the frolic, but spending time with Barbie is very special too. She is like a ray of sunshine on a cloudy day," Rebeka said.

"She is like their second mamm. She is a lot older than her years. We believe it is because of the trials she has dealt with. That has made her so special. We all marvel at her patience with children as well as with most things she goes through. I truly do not know what I would do without her. I have to remind the older ones that Barbie does twice what they do on most any given day. I let them know they should be ashamed of themselves. They do not do the work girls their age should without a fuss. Paula and Mary are so close in age they are almost like twins. It is just that my Barbie never tires nor does she complain. It always shows how God is working in her. She is always giving thanks for the wunderbaar gut life God gave her. She is grateful for everything and is never needy," Ellie said as she looked out the window watching Barbie entertain the little one.

"I believe the other girls don't understand the relationship Barbie has with God," Rebeka stated.

They all kept working and listened to Ellie. Martha and her girls arrived and joined in with everyone setting up the last few things needed. Others were coming down the lane in their buggies, and Ellie needed to greet them.

"Rachael, we are so happy you could come today." Ellie hugged her gently, seeing the pain in Rachael's eyes.

"I wouldn't have missed this event even if it meant my menfolk had to carry me in here. I want to see and be as much a part of Lucas's wedding as I can be. God will get me through," Rachael said with a smile. She didn't want to give up too much information at that point. Her two best friends needed to know first.

"Did your mamm come with you?" Ellie asked.

"She told me to go have fun and not to worry about her. She has been such a blessing to all of us," Rachael stated.

"Ach, enough talk about us." Rachael laughed. "Let's get busy on that quilt. Oh, Paula, there you are. I love this wedding ring pattern you picked out," Rachael said as she put her arm around her, "I know God will bless your marriage to my son. However, both you and Lucas need to put God first in all things. Always remember to ask for God's will to be done not yours."

The ladies enjoyed visiting and stitching until midafternoon. The quilt turned out more beautiful than Paula thought possible. She felt thankful Rachael was there to join in on the frolic, as it would always be a reminder to her when she looked at the quilt over the years to come.

After lunch, Martha and Rebeka had a few moments alone. "Rebeka, have you given further thought to writing to Kathleen?"

"Jah I did. But after praying more about it, I chose to put it from my mind. After our conversation, I have to admit you were right. I am trying to keep them apart, and that is not fair to Jacob. I think it worried me about them getting together and him taking her to Ohio. Now it is in the Lord's hands. However, in talking to Lisa, I learned that Jacob's mamm's maiden name was Miller and had married a Yoder. So maybe Kathleen is Jacob's aunt by marriage. Anyway, I decided not to send the letter. Maybe it is time we try mending some fences, but maybe the first step should come from my sister. Kathleen never joined church here, so she never went under the Bann. I believe it is up to her to reach out to us."

"I know Laura is interested in Jacob, She doesn't hide her feelings well. My fear is Laura's rebellious nature. Her daed and I are going to talk to her again before she starts going to the singings," Rebeka offered.

"Abby is worried about her also. They are very close, and of course Abby never tells us anything they talk about. I just heard Abby mumbling about her worries. I heard Laura's name, and it seemed Abby was praying for her. I don't believe Abby thought anyone was within earshot," Martha said.

"The girls will be through with school in two weeks. We will all gather to watch them receive their certificates and have our annual potluck. Abby's birthday is in a week; she turns sixteen and will be caught up with Laura. Those two remind me of us, my friend," Martha and Rebeka laughed and shook their heads.

"If we could only keep them from doing some of the things we did at their age. They would not have to go through the pain it causes," Rebeka sighed. Martha still had no clue as to the real truth about Rebeka going to Ohio.

"Laura and Abby had a good time in town yesterday. Laura came busting through the door none too soon. She barely made it on time to start her chores. As out of breath as she was, I am sure she must have run all the way from your place. Did Abby do her mumbling and praying for Laura last evening? I could not distinguish what the smell on Laura was. I gave her a kiss just to see. I have my hands full with that girl. She just had her sixteenth birthday a little over a week ago and has not yet been given permission to attend the singings. I never worried about Mary. Even though she is staying out late most evenings now, it is her sweet spirit that is always there reassuring me all is well. Mary is not my headstrong one," Rebeka confided.

"I am hoping Abby will be there with Laura to help her make the right choices. She is not afraid to speak her mind to Laura. I have heard that on more than one occasion. They are always just out of earshot; however, I see that look she gives Laura when she is talking. Ach, maybe it is a look not only of concern but of stern love, like a parents' love for a child. It makes me laugh when I see this, as Abby is the younger of the two. In some ways though, she seems to be years ahead. I am not saying that to be boastful, just observant. She does that here at times with her older siblings. And they get so mad at her, but usually, she is right in what she tells them. When they stop and think about it, they end up seeing her point of view.

"Abby's heart is to serve the Lord first. And then she wants to be a gut wife. She is making things and sticking them away for the future. As she finishes something, she looks it over with that critical eye of hers, and decides if it is gut enough to sell or if it is going into her box of stored things. I guess it is fun for me to watch my children without them knowing I do. Well, my friend, I need to be heading home. How about you?"

"Jah, it is that time all right. Better gather up my two girls and do the same. I am going to say my good-byes on my way out. I for sure want to see Rachael before I leave," Rebeka added.

The two women gathered up their baking dishes putting them into their own baskets. They got the attention of their girls, who finished packing the last few items and took them to the buggies.

"Rachael, I wanted to come tell you how wunderbaar gut it is to see you here today. You are in my prayers, and please do not hesitate to let us know if there is anything we can do to help you." Rebeka gently hugged her.

"Prayers are exactly what my family and I both need at this point. However, this is Paula's day, and it has been such a gut one for her. Let's just give thanks to God for each day we are able to spend with our loved ones." Rachael smiled sweetly.

"We will be praying for you and your family," Rebeka replied. She didn't know what Rachael's problems were, though she plainly saw she was thin and pale.

"I would love to have you and Martha over. We could visit in private. Thank you for the prayers though," Rachael ended with that smiling.

Mary had gotten both baskets in the buggy and the horse hitched up by the time Laura exited the house. "Might have been nice had you given me a helping hand, little sister. What have you been doing? I saw you and Abby slip off by yourselves right after lunch. Were you helping Abby with some chores?" Mary asked.

Rebeka was almost there, and Laura didn't want her mamm hearing her. "Ach mei! Mary, you are just too nosy as far as I am concerned. I am never allowed to question you about your rumschpringe!" Laura turned and greeted her mamm as if nothing had been said.

Mary was stunned at her sister's demeanor. She could never remember Laura acting out in such an ugly way. *What are we going to do with her?* Mary thought, shaking her head.

After rounding everyone up, they headed down the lane. Each lady there that day thanked God for their time of fellowship. They felt truly blessed to be so close, like an extended family. They all loved each other as God would have them to.

Mary thought about Romans 12:9: "Let love be without hypocrisy. Abhor what is evil. Cling to what is good," and Romans 12:10: "Be kindly affectionate to one another with brotherly love, in honor giving preference to one another." Mary felt they should love one another as the Lord loved everyone. She felt the love of the Lord as they headed home.

∞

Chapter 9

Mamm took the reins, and they headed home. Rebeka thought she detected tension between the two older girls. Mary, being the oldest, sat beside her in the front, chatting away about the fun she experienced at the frolic. Mary knew in the near future there would be frolics for her wedding quilt. Laura, however, didn't utter a word to any of them, just sat very quiet. She didn't feel like talking to anyone, and she became even moodier on the ride on the ride home.

Laura felt her family did not understand her. She and Mary did have a few unkind words toward each other, but Laura thought Mary was bossy and nosy. *Who does she think she is asking me about my whereabouts? I can't ask Mary about the time she spends with her beau or friends. Well, they should allow me to have the same privileges.* She wanted her own way. She would not get into trouble. Or so she thought.

As the wagon entered the yard, Daed came out of the barn. He greeted all of his girls and helped them down. He noticed the sour look on Laura's and Mary's faces. Just as he was about to ask what was going on, Rebeka caught his eye and shook her head no. After they had unloaded everything and had taken it inside, Rebeka took her husband off to the side and told him that words had been exchanged between the girls. She explained she hadn't heard the conversation so was in the dark about what had been said. Laura didn't realize her mamm had seen the exchange between herself and Mary.

"Ach mei, Abraham, we are going to have our hands full with Laura. She is starting to worry everyone who cares about her. She's barely started her rumschpringe and doesn't have our permission to attend the singings yet. We need to keep her in our prayers at all times. Not that we don't do that anyway, but right now, it is more crucial given her attitude toward all of us. We can't tolerate her behavior."

"Jah, my liewi, I agree with you. In town Tuesday, I saw her and Abby with some Englischer kids. Some of them looked pretty scruffy." Abraham added.

"You didn't say anything about this to me, why not? Did you say anything to Laura or Abby?"

"I said nothing. However, I am not happy with her choice of friends, but you know it is our way to let them experience some of the world. I want to leave this to our heavenly Father as our beliefs tell us to. I believe Abby, the level headed one of the two, would be more apt to tell Laura to stop acting out. You know how Abby is; she is too strong willed to get mixed up with the wrong kids. Anyway, you know the rules about the running around period as well as I do. I hate this time; I wish the elders would do away with it. It does nothing for our young people and we lose too many of our kids that way to the world," Abraham grumbled.

As Laura entered her room there sat Mary on the bed waiting to speak with her.

"Laura, we need to talk. Do you think being in your rumschpringe entitles you to act like you can run over everyone and do whatever you want? After all you haven't been given permission to attend the singings yet. That won't happen until school is out. We still live under our parents' roof, and they still pay for our food, so they deserve our respect. You behave as if you are the only one who matters. When I asked you earlier about you and your friends, I wasn't trying to be nosy. I was just trying to show you I care about what goes on in your life. When you need to talk, I am here for you. What do you think sisters are for?" Mary smiled, trying to lighten the air in the room.

"I have plenty of friends, thank you," Laura said. "And I do show our parents respect. So just leave me alone. School will be out soon, and after my rumschpringe is in full swing, none of you can tell me who I can or cannot hang out with." With that Laura turned and ran out of the room, fled down the stairs and out the front door. She felt so frustrated and just knew in her mind no one understood her.

After Laura ran out of the house, she decided to go to Abby's house and see if she wanted to go into town. As she approached, she saw Abby by the house. "Abby, how about us going into town? Do you feel up to the walk?" Laura asked.

"Jah, sure, I would love to go. So you are not mad at me anymore?" Abby's face perked up at the invitation.

"No, I couldn't stay mad at you. After all, you are my best friend." Laura put her arm around Abby's shoulders.

The girls hugged and started off down the lane toward town. Neither girl told her parents where they were going.

The two had a nice visit at the Soda Shoppe. Laura seemed to be her old, sweet self. Abby enjoyed this Laura who could be so nice when she wanted to.

The girls were still chatting away when the Englischer kids walked in. Abby wanted to run as fast as she could, but they spotted Laura and walked toward their table. Larry didn't even ask if he could sit down, he just sat down.

"Why hello, how are you?" Laura asked, her eyes sparkling.

"Oh, we're just fine. How are you and ... what's your friend's name again? Gabby?" Larry asked with a smirk on his face.

"My name is Abby, thank you very much. And you may address me when asking about me," she said with a look of exasperation.

"Oh, well excuse me for being polite."

"You call that polite? Were you raised by wolves?" Abby wanted to know.

At that point, Laura stepped in to keep the words from getting any worse. Laura could tell at this point that Abby and Larry didn't like each other. This would make it hard friends with both of them and doing things together.

"So what are you up to?" Laura asked.

"Not much at the moment. How about you two, if I'm allowed to ask?" Larry said, staring at Abby, challenging her to say something.

"Just wanted to come to town to get out for a little while," Laura smiled sweetly.

The time passed quickly. Before Laura and Abby realized it, it was ten o'clock and dark. At that point Abby panicked, jumped up from her seat, and started pulling on Laura to get going. The girls quickly said good-bye, ran out the door, and down Main Street toward home. Abby could only imagine how upset their parents would be.

As they were running for home Abby asked Laura if she thought it made her fit in trying to sound like the Englischer kids.

"I like the way they sound. What does it matter?"

"Because it makes you sound as though you are trying to be part of their world, and that is not how we were raised. It is not our way to be of their world," Abby stated emphatically.

They parted at Abby's lane without a single word coming from her best friend. It hurt Abby to see Laura want to be a part of that world.

Laura continued running as fast as she could knowing she would be in so much trouble. She hadn't told her parents she was leaving, and she hadn't been there to help with chores.

When each of the girls entered their own homes their parents were in the sitzschtupp (living room) waiting. Because the parents had not given the girls permission for that night's excursion, both girls were in big trouble. Their parents were not going to let this matter go unnoticed. Spare the rod and spoil the child.

Laura's parents thought that her attitude had started changing even before her birthday party. All too subtle at first, but Laura's parents realized they wouldn't be getting through Laura's rumschpringe as easily as they had Mary's.

When Laura entered the living room, her parents didn't mince words. They sat Laura down told her she would not be leaving the property except to go to school and they would expect her to come straight home. After Laura learned about her punishment they sent her to bed.

"Mary is very eager to settle down, where on the other hand, Laura is a free spirit. Laura's strong desire to explore the world that we are to have no part of will be her downfall. She does not hold to the Scripture,

"We are to be as strangers and pilgrims passing through this world." It also says, "Come out from among them and be ye separate saith the Lord." But with a bit of discipline and a lot of prayer, we may just get her through this," Rebeka shared with her husband.

"Jah, I have to agree with everything you said. I think her punishment for her thoughtlessness of not informing us of her outing will temper her attitude some. I hope," said her daed with worry all across his face.

"How have Martha and Aaron managed with Abby?" Abe wondered out loud.

"Ach, I think they went light on her as she was only trying to keep Laura out of trouble if possible. Abby has no desire to be involved with the group of young Englischer kids. Martha said as much yesterday while we were at the frolic and we had a moment alone."

"Well, she did take off earlier without permission, according to Aaron," Abraham said, reflecting on the visit from Aaron and Martha.

Laura was not very happy with the punishment she had received for her behavior of late and didn't think it fair. She saw nothing wrong with the way she had been behaving. *Well, I will show them.*

Abby, on the other hand, knew she had deserved her punishment she received. She knew it should have been even worse than she got. She had gone out with no thought of letting anyone know where she was going. *I must remember to let someone know next time. It is not fair to worry our loved ones. God, please forgive me of my sins, and please give me the wisdom I need to help Laura.*

∞

Chapter 10

Rachael, Allie, and Marty arrived home late that afternoon from the frolic. Rachael had winced at every breath she took, but spending the day with Paula and her friends and of course God had made it possible for her to tolerate the grueling pain. She could not tolerate her pain any more that day as the level peaked hours ago. She could not tolerate it any more without her medication that is. However, taking more of the pain medication nauseated her as well as making her groggy. It would not help the situation when Joseph came in to talk with her before dinner. The other pills that were supposed to counteract the nausea weren't working very well. She went into the living room and sat on the sofa.

"Mamm, are you all right?" Allie asked gently.

"Jah, Allie, I am just worn out from our excursion. We did have a gut time with our friends, don'tcha think?" Rachael smiled, trying to reassure Allie. "Would you get me that little wooden box by my bed and a glass of water?"

"I'll be right back with both. Is there anything else?"

"No Allie, that will be just fine." Rachael laughed, trying to lighten the mood. She did not want to worry her sweet daughter.

Marty had finished unloading the wagon with the help of her daed and brooders from their trip to the frolic. Then her brooders took the horse and wagon to the barn.

As Rachael laid there thinking, her thoughts went to what Joseph and her needed to finish this evening before dinner about their decisions. *It is time we tell the family, especially our kinner. We just can't wait any longer. It is this front we are putting up that is almost as hard on me as the illness itself.*

"Here you are, Mamm." Allie handed the box to her mamm and set a glass of water on the side table. "I am going to see what Mammi wants me to do for dinner. After last night's dinner, I had better check with her before I start on anything." Allie laughed. "Mammi sure is a live wire here of late. She always helps us with all the chores, but lately, she seems to be taking over, seeing to it that everything is done. Not that I mind the help. She is such a gut cook. And Marty is getting better at making those pies than I am. I believe that is her specialty." Allie chuckled as she went to the daadi haus to see her mammi.

"Ach, is it that time already?" Mammi asked as she looked up at the clock. "Did you girls and your mamm have a gut time at the frolic Allie?" Mammi wanted to know.

"Jah, we did. I am worried about Mamm, though. She is sitting in the living room, and she looks rather pale. I wish she and Daed would tell us what is going on with her."

"I think you worry too much, Allie girl. It would not surprise me if Joseph and Rachael didn't sit us all down after dinner tonight and tell us. I believe they might have told us last night, except your mamm was tuckered out from preparing for the frolic. She needed a day to rest up."

"Mammi, you are so wise. I always feel better after sharing my heart's troubles with you. Letting go and letting God is what you say I need to do. However, I don't know what I am letting go of." Allie still had that look of concern on her pretty face.

"God does, Allie girl. He is in control. Always remember that. If we give our problems to God and try not to dwell on them, they seem to get fixed in one manner or another. They are not always fixed in the way we would like them to be, but God does know what is best for us, my liewi." Mammi tried to reassure Allie. "Come help me finish up with dinner so your mamm and daed can spend the time they need by themselves. It will take your mind off your worries." Mammi hugged Allie around the shoulder and led her to the main house.

After Joseph and the boys had helped Marty unload the wagon, he turned to them, "Since the horse is unhitched and the wagon is put away, I am going in to sit with your mamm for a while."

The boys looked at each other and back at their daed. The look on their faces told Joseph he needed to say something more.

"Tonight, after dinner, we will have that meeting if your mamm isn't too tired from going to the frolic. Please go on with your chores, and we will call you when dinner is just about on the table." Joseph gave them a smile.

The Lord had been working on his heart the last few days. He felt he could deal with the illness of his wife a little better that day. He had spent some of the day just talking to Jesus, as Rachael had encouraged him to do.

Maybe there is something to having Jesus right beside me, he thought. When he first started talking to God and His Son, it didn't come easy for him. He had to learn to say the prayers out loud working in total privacy. He practiced every time he thought about it the last couple days. When he would find himself alone, he would just start talking to Jesus as if He were right there. That is what Rachael did, and it seemed so easy for her. But as Rachael reminded him, she had done that for a while.

Joseph entered the house to find Allie and Mammi working away. Rachael was lying down. He tried being quiet hoping she was resting. As he approached, she lifted her head. He saw the pill box beside her and knew she had needed to take more of her pain medication.

"Are you in more pain than usual today?" Joseph asked as he sat down beside his wife.

"Jah, but then our outing did make me tired. I think we need to go upstairs so we can have some privacy," Rachael said softly.

Joseph helped Rachael upstairs and gently helped her to the bed.

"Have you decided to have our family meeting tonight after dinner?" Rachael asked.

"Jah, I have been praying most of the day and speaking with our Lord. As you said, it really does seem to ease my heart. I had no idea I could find such peace in talking with Jesus. I am ready to accept Jesus as my Lord and Savior. Would you lead me through the sinner's prayer?

The last few nights we have been going through the Bible showed me what I must do," Joseph's face had softened.

"Ach mei! This is such wunderbaar gut news for my heart. Please hand me my new Bible, I have the sinner's prayer written in there." Rachael grinned from ear to ear. She knew the Lord had done a mighty work in her husband.

Rachael and Joseph prayed to the Lord to go before them. They read the sinner's prayer together. Joseph gave a prayer of thanksgiving to Christ for accepting him into His family. He knew he would continue to work on his personal relationship with Jesus, his Lord and Savior.

After reassuring Rachael he would be ready to talk to their family about not only her illness but also about Jesus, they descended the stairs.

Rachael had never been involved in helping anyone say the sinner's prayer. She felt as giddy as Ruthie on the day she invited Jesus into her heart. She remembered when she had asked Ruthie to lead her through the prayer. Ruthie had been giddy with joy for her. Now she understood those feelings Ruthie felt that day.

Through the depths of darkness, now there is light. *'Father, if it be Your will, please give us the strength where we can show those we love how important and wonderful it can be. If we can be that light for Jesus, my life here on earth will have more meaning. Whatever time You have given me, Father, please let me be your humble servant. Help Joseph and me to guide our family closer to You.*

Joseph liked the feelings he got when he used the outward prayers. He had to admit he felt washed as clean as the first snow before anyone has walked on it. "Rachael, we still must keep what goes on in our house private. Help me explain the importance of this to our children. It is not that I am ashamed of my Lord and Savior by any means. I am just not ready to be shunned or placed under the Bann, nor do I want that happening to the rest of our family. With your mamm already knowing the end results if this got out helps me not to worry so much about them. Are we in agreement on this?" Joseph asked while helping her to sit up.

"Jah Joseph, for now I will agree with you," Rachael was thinking it would not be long before it got out among the People anyway. "Joseph, the nausea pills are in the pill box, please hand me the other half. I thought a half would be enough, but it isn't. The doctors said my not wanting to eat has a lot to do with being nauseated, which comes from not only my pain from the cancer but the medications. I promised them this week I would try to eat a little better."

"It takes a while before the pill takes effect, however, by the time we eat it should be working. The doctors also said the nausea would subside in a few days as my body adjusts to the stronger dosage of the pain medication. Too much moving around also makes it worse until my body adjusts. I hate having to heap all this on you. So, I am stopping there about my illness. We have far more important things to discuss." Rachael smiled silently thanking God for Joseph's salvation.

Joseph retrieved the pill and poured her some water. He worried about all these medications. In all his life he didn't remember being around any medications. He thought for a moment and realized he must turn his fears over to God as Rachael does.

Allie knocked softly and opened the door. "Dinner is ready."

Joseph thanked her and helped Rachael down the stairs and to the table. Everyone was quietly waiting on them. After helping Rachael to her chair, he took his place at the head of the table. Since all were seated they held hands around the table and waited on their daed.

Joseph looked at Rachael and she nodded her head, yes. Her hand in his gave him the reassurance he needed to say the evening prayer out loud. They had decided he would tell the children first he would be saying grace out loud before he started, this way they wouldn't be shocked and not listen to the prayer.

"Family, as you know, your mamm and I have been spending the last few nights trying to figure out all we needed to tell you. However, tonight, I ask you to bow your heads, eyes closed, and listen carefully while I pray out loud."

The kids looked at each other and at their daed and mamm, but they obeyed. Joseph felt thankful there weren't any questions at that time. There would be plenty of those later.

"After dinner, we will get things cleaned up quickly and then will have our meeting. Your mamm and I have some things to share with you, and then will answer your questions to the best of our ability. Please be patient with me. Because as you know I am not in the habit of praying out loud, I may stumble, but God will be there to help me. *"Father, we come before you this evening asking You to bless this food to our bodies and bless the hands that prepared it. We ask You to open the hearts and minds listening to this prayer that they would accept Your Word and Your Son as Rachael and I have. We ask all this in Your Son, Jesus Christ of Nazareth's most precious name, Amen.""* Joseph looked up and smiled saying, "Let's dig in, it all looks so gut."

There was dead silence at first. None of the younger ones knew what to think. Mammi started a light conversation to ease the tension around the table. Rachael was on the verge of tears spilling down her face. They would be tears of joy; however, the others would not know that. She felt relieved her mamm stepped in to help.

"Allie, did a lot of women turn out for the gathering at Ellie's for the frolic? When you all got home, I should have asked then," Mammi inquired.

"Jah Mammi, there sure were. That quilt for Lucas and Paula is beautiful. It will be keeping them plenty warm this coming winter after they are wed. Lucas, you are a very lucky man to have found Paula, what a girl. She has enough energy in her for two or three people. I don't think I saw her one time all day sitting idle. If her fingers were not flying on the quilt, she was helping in some other way." Allie loved teasing her brother, trying to draw the look of concern off his face.

Lucas looked up, his face beet red. Embarrassed, didn't come close to how he felt. Families usually didn't bring up beds and being warm at the dinner table, especially when they were talking about people who were not wed yet. Lucas let it pass and a little smile crept to the corners of his mouth.

"Allie girl, I could not agree with you more," Mamm said. "A sweet spirit permeates the room coming from Paula. We will welcome her into our home, and you girls will have a new sister to help you. I feel blessed that Paula's family is not from here, or Lucas, you and Paula would be moving in with her family. The more here the merrier." Rachael smiled at her son.

Lucas' mind was racing. He and Paula would start their period of instruction and then be baptized into the church. *What on earth is going on?* Lucas thought to himself. He didn't want to jump to any conclusions until after he heard what his folks were going to tell them. He didn't want their family to go under the Bann, but something was awry. *Amish don't say prayers out loud, not ever!*

The meal went pleasingly well. Rachael ate as much as she could. Joseph pleaded with his eyes for her to have just a few more bites; she smiled and rubbed her tummy. Enough said.

"Let's all gather back to the table now that everything is redd up for morning," Joseph stated. He prayed to himself.

"Father, please go before me and my wife this evening. We want Your will to be done here, not ours. Please help my children and our folks to understand what it is You want them to hear and do. Give them peace about Rachael's illness and about Jesus Christ. We pray all this in Your Son's most precious name, Amen."

Joseph looked up to see everyone looking at him. His kids seemed scared. He thought it would be best to let Rachael tell them of her illness. That might better help them understand how she had come to have the peace God gave her. Joseph looked to his wife and nodded. "Would you please tell the family what the doctors have told you so far about your condition?"

"Jah, I need to, they need to know just as you did. Well kids and folks, as you probably have noticed, I have lost quite a bit of weight lately. I went to see the doctors months ago only to learn I am really sick. They did all they could to help me, but as the months went by, my illness only advanced. The doctors were unable to do anything. They gave me a choice to go outside our area and get a different kind of treatment, but they could not ensure that it would do any good, as far developed and advanced as my cancer is."

"Mamm, what is this illness?" Marty demanded.

"Please be patient with me, as telling this to my family is not easy for me. The illness I have is a form of cancer. There are many types."

As Rachael began her explanation, tears began to flow around the room. Everyone was so quiet; their faces looked as though they all might hit the floor. They shook their heads, not wanting to believe anything Rachael said. They were actually in shock. Especially Marty, who threw herself into her mamm's arms crying. "No Mamm, this can't be! Can't those doctors you have been seeing help you?"

Rachael wrapped her arms around Marty and stroked her hair. "No honey, there is nothing they can do. But we can do something. We can all pray to God to help us through this trial."

Joseph eased Marty into his arms. She felt as limp as a rag. Afraid she might put too much weight on Rachael, he held her close. He then spoke up and asked if anyone had any questions, still holding Marty close to him. Allie and her brooders were afraid to ask questions. Allie for one didn't know if they could stand to hear the answer. Allie knew she needed to know exactly what to expect, as she was the oldest girl. This would affect her life greatly.

Lucas spoke up first, "Did the doctors say how much time we have left with you?"

"They said a matter of a few weeks, that leaves it open. Let's all hope for a few months. We are going to unite this family and make it a fun time. It will do none of us any good to mope around or cry. Marty, honey, I know this is harder on you. You are my youngest, my baby, so to speak. However, now, I need you to be my big girl and be strong. We are all going to lean on God to see us through."

"God is taking you from me!" Marty screeched still crying, "How can He do that to this family? It will tear us apart Mamm! I don't even want to talk to God." Marty tore away from the clutches of her daed and fled the room. She ran upstairs and into the bedroom she shared with Allie. She didn't want to be around anyone, not right then. She needed time to think. *I'm not even out of school and am losing my mamm. All girls my age have their mamm.* She was being selfish and she knew it, but she didn't care.

The rest of the family sat waiting to see what their mamm wanted to do as far as Marty was concerned. It wasn't normal for an outburst like that in and among the Plain People. Under the circumstances, Rachael decided to let it go and explain her faith to the remaining family members. "Let's go ahead and finish with what we want to share with you and let Marty be for a while. I will sit with her and explain later in private. Joseph, do you want to lead us in another prayer before we start explaining what Jesus means to us?"

"Jah, please family, bow your heads again as we go before the Lord our God."

"Father, we come to You again in prayer. We are thanking You for letting Rachael have the strength to share her illness with us. Father, please lay Your hands upon her and give her peace and comfort in her time of need. We do give You praise, honor, and glory for bringing us closer to You. Through Rachael's illness she discovered Jesus Christ as her Lord and Savior. We are so grateful now she will be in heaven with You and Jesus, awaiting the rest of us. Please give Rachael the wisdom to tell her testimony with our children and her parents. We give thanks for all You do in our lives, Amen."

"How can you thank God for taking Mamm away from us?" John spoke with a cracking voice.

"John, I want you to listen to your mamm's testimony. Then, if you have a question, we will answer it."

"What is a testimony?" John asked.

"A testimony is the telling of how something came about and the effect it has on you. The proof your testimony is true and actual is the peace that engulfs you. It really is hard to explain until it happens to you, but that is our wish and hope. That is one thing your mamm and I have been praying about these last few nights, is that you hear her out and then pray about what she tells you. Is that fair?" Joseph asked his family.

Rachael looked around the room, everyone nodding in agreement. They would hear her out.

"Family, as you know, I have been going to Ruthie and Robert's house several times a week. When I became sick, Ruthie would not let me lift a finger to work and asked that if she paid me, could we just sit and visit and read the Bible. I saw her reach down by her sofa where she sat and pulled out this box and handed it to me. I opened it, and there inside the box was a brand new Bible." Rachael smiled reflecting back to that day. "I opened it carefully, as I wasn't sure I should have it and didn't want to damage it. Ruthie said, 'It won't break. It has been around for a long time.' So I opened it and Ruthie had written my name in the front, saying it was from her and Robert. She also wrote a few Scriptures in the front for me to refer to." Rachael said looking around the room.

"I didn't want to hurt her feelings, so, I just thanked her for it. Ruthie had been someone I confided in about my illness. She saw me on a regular basis and noticed the weight dropping off me. Her concern for me showed on her face and would ask me what the doctors had said. She is also one person who took me to the doctors on several occasions. Actually, it was Ruthie who suggested I go see the doctor in the first place."

"As the weeks went by and we read the Bible together, I listened to her pray. With each prayer, God touched my heart. Sometimes, I would catch myself praying out loud around here and would look to see if anyone had heard.

"I can't say how many months went by, but one day, God spoke right to me. I thought I was hearing things and went about by business. However, as time passed, I heard this voice speaking right to my heart. As I told your daed, John 3:16 reached out and got a hold of me. I kept hearing it over and over in my mind."

Rachael paused, took a drink, and went on. "One day not long ago, I accepted Jesus Christ as my Lord and Savior. This does not feel haughty to me, as it is what God tells us to do in the Bible. It also tells us to share the Good News of Jesus," Rachael spoke softly to her family. "Please don't judge me, but pray about it yourself. My wish for this family is that we have a study period each evening in the English Bible. I believe it is easier to understand. Now, your daed and I have another request from all of you. We want what goes on in our house to stay in our house. That means our study time in the Bible and our prayers that we as a family are going to say out loud need to remain here in our home."

"I know God can hear our silent prayers, however, the rest of us can't, and I want to hear what is on your hearts. God will not be mad at you for praying to Him out loud. He wants you to have an open relationship with Him and His Son, Jesus Christ. Please come to me or your daed with questions you might have regarding the Bible or where to find a passage. We will do our best to help each of you."

"Please pray for Marty and be kind to her. This is going to be hard on all of us but harder on her. Do any of you have anything you want to ask or add this evening before we end in prayer?" Rachael smiled at her family and tried to keep her pain to herself.

Mammi spoke up. "Daughter, I have been reading the Bible for many years myself. Your daed and I decided to keep it to ourselves that he gave me permission to read the Bible as long as I didn't go off telling anyone. Therefore, if I can be of help to our family, please have them come to me also. Rachael, I can't begin to tell you how pleased I am to hear that you and your husband have given your lives to Christ. My heart soared with joy, not that you are sick, my dear, but that we will be in heaven together."

"Ach mei, this is not a good time for me to try to decide all this, with Paula and me starting our instruction for baptism," Lucas asked. "It makes everything different. I love God and I love my parents with all my heart and I don't wish to go against the two of you. What am I to do?" He felt weary, beside himself.

"Son, we want you to pray about this first before you make any decisions. If you commit your life to Christ in the church, that is perfect. However, by our own admission of accepting Christ as our Lord and Savior is something we need to keep in our hearts and at home. Use your life as an outward example of an inward walk with Christ. We do not have to go around telling the world what goes on in our home. When we have others in our home, we will do what the bishops have instructed us to do." Rachael offered gently.

"Just pray about it and we will meet again in the morning. Your mamm looks as though she needs to lie down. I need to find your little sister and see if I can help her understand what is going on," Joseph said to Lucas and the others sitting there.

The family sat in silence while Joseph helped Rachael from the room after she gave them all kisses on her way by.

Still shaking his head, Lucas got up and went out to the barn. He did some of his best thinking in the barn. He thought this was a lot to put on Paula, and first, he needed to take it to the Lord in prayer. As he sat there in prayer, a peace came to him that was hard to explain. The peace seemed to engulf him, surround him like he actually had God's arms around him. He would follow his parents; he trusted them as he did the Lord, and he prayed Paula would do the same.

Lucas needed to talk to her and give her a choice. He knew his daed would need him more right now than ever before. With his mamm being so sick, his daed would want to spend as much time with her as possible. The workload would shift to him and his two younger brooders. One thing he knew he must do is to apologize to his parents for his selfish attitude. Here his mamm was dying, and he sat there thinking about himself and Paula. *Lord, please forgive me. Paula's heart is for You. We will just see what happens. After all, You are in control of everything.*

Allie went over to her mammi and rested her head on her shoulder. She let the tears flow down her checks. She didn't feel like talking. Her mammi patted her leg and leaned her head into Allie's.

The other two boys went to their room without saying more than a good night to the others remaining in the room.

After Joseph had settled Rachael into their bed and made sure she had her medication, he kissed her and said he would be back after trying to talk to Marty.

When Joseph knocked on the girl's bedroom door, he got no response. He opened the door to find the room empty. He went back downstairs to see if she had returned down there. When he didn't find her, he went to see if the rest of the family had seen her. When no one had, Joseph asked Allie to check the bathroom. Allie came back to say she was not in there. Joseph asked them all to help try to find her. They searched the rest of the house and then went to the barn. They found Lucas sitting on a bale of hay but no sign of Marty. Lucas said he had not heard anyone come in and he had been there for a while.

They looked at each other, all scared for their little sister. Joseph instructed them to spread out. Lucas went down to where the big oak tree hung over the creek. That low tree branch had always been a favorite place for Marty to sit and watch the creek flow by, however, this evening the branch sat bare.

The family didn't know what to do or where to look next. Marty didn't normally do anything she would get into trouble for. However, the news she had received that evening was not normal news, and she had been very upset.

They all met upstairs in their parent's bedroom and prayed for Marty's safety, leaving it in God's hands.

∞

Chapter 11

Laura became more and more agitated at the thought of being stuck on the farm for three days, and her punishment had just begun a few hours earlier. After she had assured herself the rest of the family had gone to bed, she decided to get out for a walk. Because Mary was not at home, she didn't see how she could be found out.

She went into the fields since she could not leave the property and walked for a while when she heard a young girl crying. Being this late she couldn't figure out who it would be at this time of night.

She located the girl and found it to be Marty Lapp. "What are you doing out here? Do you realize how late it is? Your parents are probably worried sick about you."

When Laura walked closer to her, Marty was so upset about her mamm that she just blurted it out. "My mamm is going to die. Why is God going to take her away from me? I hate God!" Marty sobbed.

"Here, let's take a walk, and you can tell me all about it," Laura said, taking Marty's hand and helping her up.

They walked for about an hour while Marty related every detail of her mother's illness. Laura felt so bad for Marty. She wished she could do something for her. Laura shuddered at the thought of someone so young losing her mamm.

"Ach, Marty, you should not hate God for this. It is not His fault your mamm is dying. People get sick and people die. That is the cycle of life. You just need to enjoy the time you have left with her and be strong. When you are with her, don't be sad, because it will make her sad, and she will worry."

The girls walked on for a while longer. Laura let Marty go on talking as it seemed to calm her. Then Laura told Marty about how strict her parents were being since her rumschpringe had started.

As they were winding down their conversation, they were approaching Marty's house. Laura encouraged Marty to go in and let her parents know she had returned safely and to apologize for leaving without telling anyone.

"Thank you Laura for listening I do feel much better even though I am still sad, but better," Marty tried to smile to show her appreciation. She turned and said, "I will let my parent's know I am back. I will try not to look sad. I'm not sure that is possible, but I will try. My mamm deserves better from me."

"Ach mei! That is gut to hear Marty. It will make things much easier for everyone." Laura watched as Marty went in the house, and then she walked on towards home. She thought about how sad the whole community would be when Rachael passed on. She wondered if her mamm knew about Rachael. She hadn't gone very far from the Lapp farm when she came upon Jacob.

Jacob was getting an early start on the firewood supply for winter. He stood with axe in hand ready to split the next piece. He enjoyed the cool quiet of the night, and he had permission from his Uncle Robert to be out cutting wood.

Laura, very nervous about Jacob knowing she had adventured out at that late hour approached him anyway. *Will he tell my parents?*

"Well Laura, how are ya? You should not be out this late by yourself. It is not always safe," Jacob stated kindly.

"I'll be just fine. I needed to get out of the house for a while. I love this time of night. It is so quiet; it gives me a chance to think."

"What do you need to think about alone late at night and away from your home? Is it anything I can help you with?" Jacob asked with concern.

"Ach mei, no Jacob. Nothing I wish to discuss at the moment. Thank you for asking though," Laura said sweetly.

"Laura, if I may be so bold, I would like to drive you home when I'm finished here," Jacob offered, "I will be done soon."

"That is very nice of you, denki. I do believe I will take you up on your offer," Laura replied.

The moon was shining so bright that Laura could see the features on Jacob's face. She just loved to look at him. He didn't act as though he knew he was so handsome. That made him even more appealing.

"How are you enjoying your new home Jacob?"

"I am very happy my parents let me move here. I live with a wunderbaar gut family and I have a job I love. I am learning to build with my hands, and am able to use the gifts God gave me. And now I am with a wunderbaar girl. Will you be going to the singings soon?" Jacob asked.

"Ach jah, I can't wait for the first one I am allowed to attend." Laura offered, "Will you be going?"

"I have already started, and up until now, I haven't found a girl to take riding. I know of a buggy I can borrow until I get my own," Jacob said with hope in his heart.

Laura blushed and chose to act as if she had not heard him.

Standing in the bright moon light Jacob could see her blush. He figured he may have gone just a little too far. "Well, I am all finished, so how about that ride home I promised?"

"That sounds gut. I know I should be home right now," Laura could not believe she was in the company of this nice young man. *Maybe I am getting just a wee bit to worldly. This might not be in my best interest. Here is this nice young man, and my running around may be ruining my chances with him if he were to learn of my outings with Abby.*

As they got closer to her parents' farm, Laura became very aware of how loud the wagon sounded in the still of the night. She didn't want to wake the entire household, so she asked to be let off at the end of their lane. That way, no one would know she had been out. She thought it a perfect plan.

Jacob thought it a bit odd but did as she had asked. "Will I be seeing you at the next singing then?" Jacob asked.

"Jah Jacob, it sounds like such fun!" Laura stated with a smile that nearly made Jacob go weak in the knees.

With that Laura got down and walked the rest of the way home. She entered the house, went to her room, and got herself redd up for bed. She climbed in between line dried sheets and nestled her face into the pillow case and sighed a big relief. As for her outing no one would be the wiser. She had made it. Her sister wouldn't be home for hours yet.

Unbeknownst to Laura, Mary and her beau were on the road in his courting buggy and riding in the same direction as Laura had been walking.

Mary was shocked to see her out so late, knowing she had been told not to leave the property. Well, she hoped Laura could think of a good reason for not obeying their parents. She did not want to confront her at that point; she had so little time left on this moonlit night to be with Micah. She would speak to her in the morning.

And by the grace of God He would see her through her rumschpringe. Laura needed to be turned over to God. He would be the only One to turn her around at this point in her life. *Thank you Father God for giving us the wisdom to help my sister we love so dearly......Amen.*

∞

Chapter 12

Marty let herself into the house. Trying to be as quiet as possible, she knocked softly on her parents' bedroom door. The door opened and her daed stood there with tears in his eyes. He opened his arms and Marty threw herself into them. He engulfed her with his long arms and let her cry. He gently moved her into the room so he could shut the door. They walked together over to the bed where Rachael laid worried sick about her daughter.

"Ach mei! Daughter, where on earth have you been?" Rachael demanded, "This will not be tolerated from you for any reason. Do I make myself clear?"

"Rachael please, don't discipline her right now. Marty just received some horrible news. Not that I agree with what she did, however, let's hear her out first. Marty, I think your mamm's anger comes from being scared. Is that right, my liewi?" Joseph asked kindly, looking from one to the other.

"Jah, I do suppose you are right. When a mamm gets scared for a young one and sees that young one does not have something broken or hurt, first comes the anger. I am sorry I yelled at you; however, there will be punishment for running out of here tonight. I do know you are hurting on the inside. Your heart must feel broken, jah?" Rachael said as she opened her arms to let Marty hug her.

"Ach Mamm, I am so sorry for running out of here. I didn't even think it would worry you until Laura told me I shouldn't worry my parents," Marty said.

"Laura?" Rachael questioned.

"Jah, Laura Knapp. She found me in their field where I was crying. We talked for quite some time. Laura listened to what made me so sad and then encouraged me to come home, she then walked with me making sure I was safe. Again, I am so sorry for making such a scene. Laura did help me see that it was not God's fault for you being sick. I will try to help in as many ways as I can. Maybe the doctors are wrong and you will have more time with us than they think." Marty looked at both parents with a hopeful expression on her face.

"You must understand that in this, Laura was right. It is not God's fault your mamm is sick. However, the doctors have done many tests, and your mamm is not going to get better here on earth. We have a lot more to explain to you than your mamm's sickness. We want to wait until tomorrow to go into what the family talked about after you fled the room," Joseph said.

Joseph and Rachael were so grateful to Laura for encouraging Marty to come home. They wondered why Marty had gone to the Knapp field, but it was better than some places she could have ended up.

Rachael knew she would have to tell Rebeka and Martha tomorrow with everything that is transpiring about her illness. They had been friends for as long as Rachael could remember, and they deserved that much. She knew she didn't want them hearing about it through the grapevine. However, she would only share her illness for the time being. That would be enough for her friends to handle in one setting.

She imagined that with Laura knowing, Rebeka may be privy to the knowledge already. She should have told them before this, but she needed to first tell her family. God would work it all out. "Since Marty shared my illness with Laura, I am going to have the ladies over tomorrow so I can tell them, it is only fair. We are such close friends," Rachael softly stated.

"So my liewi, is it alright with you to tell them about my illness?" Rachael asked.

"Ach, you don't need my permission. We can send Jonas over on Babe right after breakfast to give each an invitation. I will instruct him not to get caught up in conversations with the menfolk at either place. He can be polite and then tell them he is on an errand for his mamm and that his work is awaiting him back home. That should keep him from spilling his grief to anyone." Joseph felt that Jonas was safe on Babe, who had been trained beyond being just a buggy horse.

"I'll write a short missive to each he can deliver. That way, he won't have to explain himself to them. It should speed him up as well." Rachael chuckled at the thought of Jonas and his antics. "He can wait for their answers."

"I think that is a right gut idea," Joseph said.

"Denki Joseph. You are changing right before my eyes. There is a softening about you that could only come from Jesus. These changes fill me with joy."

"Rachael, I am thinking we should keep Marty home from school for the rest of this week. Not only will she be a help here to Allie and Sarah, but can be here for you too. At some point tomorrow, we need to share our faith with her. With the rest of the children knowing everything, it is bound to be discussed among them. It makes sense with our children being so close they would share the sorrows of their hearts. Marty is going to have a hard time with the illness by itself. When we share Jesus and tell her it is a must to keep our faith here at home, she is going to need time to digest it all. Our children are well behaved and have never done anything we have asked them not to do, so I am confident we can trust them. And if it does get out, we will deal with that too. However, for now, let's pray we keep it here at home," Joseph stated.

"You are such a gut husband, I feel blessed to be a part of your life," Rachael whispered softly.

"Rachael, don't get me wrong, I am struggling with this myself. It is all so new. I can only imagine how Marty is also going to struggle." Joseph added.

"Tomorrow, I will sit with Marty and tell her about Jesus. It will take a while, so I agree with you about her staying home with me," Rachael said.

"We are so fortunate to have the help from your parents, especially your mamm. In all my years of knowing them, and with them living the Old Order Amish, how your daed gave your mamm permission to read an English Bible I will never understand, even in the confines of their own bedroom. I have been thinking on that since you first told me your mamm helped you with your walk with Christ."

"Not one time in all these years has there been a hint of her giving her life to Jesus, asking Him to be her Lord and Savior. Now that I think back over all the years I have known her, she has always been a Godly woman. She has shown by her actions, not her words, that Jesus has always lived in her heart. With Mamm reading the Bible has made it a lot easier in our house. You are right, you know."

"What do you mean, I am right?" Rachael's curiosity was piqued.

"Well, our outward walk shows the love of Christ through our daily living, while our inward walk is more personal, as you were telling Lucas. Once you explained it all to me and I prayed about it, such a feeling of peace came over me. I am still very sad about your leaving us behind, however, it does make it much easier knowing someday we will all be together again in Heaven." Joseph went to sit on the side of the bed and took Rachael in a loving embrace.

"Always remember Joseph, this is all God's doing. Not any of this is me, and I always want to make that clear. Don't misunderstand me, I am overcome with joy being allowed to witness your acceptance of Christ as the Son of God and you're asking Jesus into your heart. If I took my last breath tonight, I could rest assured you could and would help our family from here forward."

Joseph looked at Rachael with love in his eyes, however, he couldn't tell her for sure he would be able to live up to what she thought he could do. Being a new believer left a lot of doubt in his mind. His eyes showed his feelings.

"Joseph please, these thoughts I have need to be shared with someone. You are my husband. Who else would I share the complete thoughts of my heart with? Please, don't make me walk on eggshells. Never knowing if I can share with you would put such a strain on our time left. Be that one person I can share everything in the world with, well, besides Christ," Rachael said with a smile.

"Ach, I am so sorry. Please forgive me for being selfish. I know God does not want me to act that way. If I am stumbling in my walk already, how hard is it going to be for our kinner?" Joseph asked with worry lines across his forehead.

"Romans 3:23 tells us, 'For all have sinned and fall short of the glory of God.' We are going to stumble, all of us. And will continue to stumble until we receive our new bodies in Christ. Don't be so hard on yourself or our children. The just will live by faith. We both have a lot to learn. That is why we must have our family devotion time each evening as we have always done. The only difference will be our using the English Bible. There is a verse also in Romans 1:16, where Paul says, 'For I am not ashamed of the gospel of Christ, for it is the power of God to salvation for everyone who believes.' Jesus tells us that we are to share the Good News of Him and His resurrection."

Rachael knew Joseph had much to absorb as far as the Bible was concerned. She thought they both should get some rest. "Would you pray for us before we turn in for the night Joseph? It seems to come easier to pray the more we do it."

As Joseph ended their nightly prayer, they were holding hands. She gave his hands a squeeze and opened her eyes to look into his. The love that showed in his face is a memory she would take with her. That is if such a thing happened like that. Having so many unanswered questions herself, she realized she needed to ask Robert and Ruthie about some of them. She could only imagine how her whole family felt the stress of all she and Joseph had told them so far.

∞

Chapter 13

Thursday dawned warm and beautiful. Abby felt guilty over being so thoughtless as far as her parents were concerned. She decided to seek her mamm; she needed to see just how upset she was. She found her at the clothesline.

"Gut morning Mamm. Are you doing alright on this beautiful day?" Abby asked.

"I am doing fine my liewi, and you?" Martha smiled.

As Abby started to speak she could not help but burst into tears. She wrapped her arms around her mamm and hugged her tight.

"Daughter, what is this all about?" The love being ever so evident in her mamm's voice made Abby feel all the worse for her actions.

"Ach Mamm, I am so sorry about my thoughtlessness. I never meant to upset or scare you. I love you, and I love our way of life. I would never do anything to jeopardize my standing with the People. My reason for my behavior, although not an excuse, is motivated by my love for my friend. I want to make sure Laura gets through her rumschpringe period with as little trouble as possible. Mamm, Laura has so much anger in her right now. I am not sure what to do to help her except be there." Abby was pouring her heart out.

"Ach, my little one, you must leave her in God's hands and trust in Him. He will get you and Laura through this time. I know it is hard to just let someone follow a way that you know is destructive to them. However, she is in God's loving care, and even though she might not be doing God's will, He can use this time to teach Laura. In the end let us pray she will have a stronger walk with our Heavenly Father." Martha hoped she was offering Abby hope.

"Mamm, may I stay close to Laura to help her? I will be very careful and won't do anything that would go against our ways."

"Jah, you may, but if at any point you fear for yourself or Laura, get help however you need to do it. There are a lot of Godly people in town, and if need be, go to them if you are in danger."

"But Mamm, we are taught to keep the Englischers out of our affairs."

"Daughter, you must promise me you will do this if you are in any danger. It will give me comfort if the need arises. After all, those are Englischers' kids Laura wants to be around, which will only lead to trouble. There are nice Englischers who go to church." Martha looked deep into Abby's eyes. They were the road maps to her soul, and Abby's were so clear. She knew who her daughter's heart belonged to.

"I will Mamm, I promise. I love you with all my heart. You are the best mamm a girl could have." With that Abby ran off to do her chores. She thought about what her mamm had said about the Englischers. She was relieved to know she had permission to call upon them if she felt the need. She decided to do some praying before things got out of control. *God, I know I have started off on the wrong path. Please forgive me. I asked You, Father, to guide my ways. I will try to always do Your will. I also seek wisdom in dealing with Laura and her Englischer friends. Let us both be a light to them. Please be with Laura as she makes her decisions. Show her what You have for her, and I will pray she will do the right thing according to Your will and not of her own flesh. Help me to be that friend she needs right now. Give me the strength to resist Satan and his deception, Amen.* Abby had gone to her Father on bended knee. She knew He was there, she felt His presence and a strong feeling of peace. She gave herself a hug as though it came from the Father and smiled.

Mary, despite being tired from being out late with Micah, got up early. She wanted to take Laura aside and have a talk with her. Mary felt disturbed with Laura for having been out that late, not to mention going against their parents rules. Mary didn't understand, Laura knew she was grounded to the farm for three days but had disobeyed their parents anyway. Where this disobedience was coming from Mary couldn't figure out. She loved her sister and didn't want to see her in trouble. *Lord, what can we do to help her?* She didn't want to fight with Laura. *Lord, please go before me.*

"Laura, I want to talk to you," Mary caught up with Laura.

"Jah? What can I do for you?" Laura asked haughtily.

"I saw you out last night walking home. What were you doing off the farm? You know you were not to leave the farm at all. Those were our parents' orders." Mary stated firmly.

"Well, if you must know, I walked Marty home last night," Laura offered and went on, "I became so irritated at being grounded to our property that I decided to take a walk in our field. That's when I found Marty sobbing her eyes out and I could not let her walk home alone. She told me about her mamm being sick and my heart ached for her, and that is why I left our property. So you see, you don't have to always be worrying about me and my whereabouts."

"Ach sister, I am so sorry for assuming the worst, I should not have interfered. I am so very sorry, will you forgive me?"

"Ach jah, I will. Let's not say another word about this."

"Denki Laura, you are such a gut sister." Mary gave her a hug.

Laura could not have felt guiltier if she had tried. She had just lied to her sister, something they had never done before. She stood shaking her head at her actions. Then she shrugged her shoulders and down the stairs she went. She knew Mary would not say anything to her parents now.

Mary was uneasy even with Laura's explanation.
Father, please watch over my sister. I fear she does not know what she is up against.

∞

Chapter 14

The sun was shining brightly when Rachael opened her eyes. Her family had let her sleep in. The outing to the frolic two days earlier had worn her out more than she had thought it would. She could never remember not being the first one up. The different aromas coming from downstairs—bacon, coffee, and sweets of some sort—made her tummy growl. *My tummy is craving those smells. But she knew she couldn't eat them.*

She didn't want her family fussing so much. She needed to make her family think she was eating, so a few scrambled eggs and a piece of dry toast should appease them. *Please Father, help me to be that shining light for You in my last days. Forgive my sins.*

Rachael made her way downstairs, dressed and redd up for the day. She needed to spend time with Marty alone. Joseph had told her last night that he would tell Marty she would be staying home the rest of the week. When she entered the kitchen; her mamm, Allie, and Marty were busy doing one thing or another. They didn't hear her come in at first she had been so quiet.

"Gut morning to all of you," Rachael said as cheerfully as she could muster. She looked around and everything was running smoothly. They really didn't need her as much as she had thought. She knew they were capable of doing it all; but she had been doing it herself for so many years she felt it would not get done correctly if she was not there. *Well, if I don't feel full of myself.* She laughed and felt foolish. *They will be just fine without me.*

Marty was the first one to her side, "What can we get for you, Mamm?"

"Ach, some scrambled eggs and a piece of dry toast sounds so gut. That will do me this morning, denki for asking. Did you all eat your breakfast while I lay in bed? What a lazy one I am today!" Rachael said giggling.

"Daed and the boys went to get a daybed for you. He thought you might enjoy being down here with us and could lie down when you needed to," Marty put in. "We moved things around this morning so the daybed would fit right next to the kitchen. That way, you can be close to us while we are working in here. We want you to be as comfortable as possible. Daed had a gut talk with us this morning before they left for town. If you want anything, please call me," Marty said, mustering up the biggest smile she could find, though her heart was shattered.

"Ach mei, Marty, what a change in you overnight." Rachael said with tears in her eyes.

"Mamm, my talk with Laura last night and my prayers with God throughout the night left me feeling stronger. I do feel as though I can be that strong girl you need me to be. I am sorry I shared your illness with Laura last night. I just needed to talk to someone, and when she found me, I just couldn't help telling her. I am sorry I ran out of here, and I know my family is who I should have been talking to. Will you forgive me?"

"Marty, you are my child, and of course I forgive you, had you done something wrong. Honey, you were distraught. Being scared when we could not find you, I did lash out at you, however, that is only a mamm's reaction. One day you will know what I am talking about when you have children of your own." Rachael said as she hugged her daughter.

Joseph, Lucas, and John came in through the front door with a beautifully handmade wooden daybed that had come from the Miller Furniture Store. It had been a regular twin bed, but with a few changes, Robert had made it into a daybed. The carvings on the legs were very attractive and usually not something that would appear in an Amish home. However, because Robert had his shop in town and selling to

Englischers, some of his projects were crafted with more detail. Robert would not take any money for the daybed once Joseph told Robert it would be sitting in their living room for Rachael to rest on during the day.

They got it all set up and by the time that was done and Sarah brought in the bedding and a beautiful new quilt she had been working on for the top. She also brought several pillows with newly stitched cases that matched the spread.

Rachael thought she knew most things her mamm worked on, but not to her recollection did she remember any of these. *They must be things mamm worked on in the evenings after she went to the daadi haus*, she thought. Her mouth opened farther than she realized, and Joseph walked over to tell her she was going to catch a fly. He laughed, and Rachael shut her mouth. She then laughed also as she hugged them all. *How thoughtful of them all to want to make me as comfortable as possible.*

"Joseph, where is Jonas? Is he not with you?"

"I sent him over to give your missives to both ladies, and he should be back any moment. He left when we did, and considering the work Robert did on the bed while we waited, he should have been back already. Maybe he ran across someone who needed a helping hand. We will give him a few more minutes."

They moved out of the way as Allie, Sarah, and Marty made up the daybed. Breathtaking beauty is what Rachael saw. She didn't know if she could lie on it for fear she would mess it all up. She also felt very thankful to God. Because of Him, her whole family had opened their minds, allowing His work to be done.

"Mamm, Daed, do you have a few minutes where I might have some time to ask both of you a few questions before your friends get here," Lucas asked.

"Sure son, what is on your mind?" Joseph asked.

He looked around the room waiting for the others standing around reason to find something else to do to give them some privacy.

"Well, after praying and thinking last night in the barn, I thought it best to include Paula in on our family circle," Lucas said. "She will soon be my wife, and I don't want to keep things from her. Would it not be best to give her the choice to live as we do before joining The Old Order Amish?" Lucas scratched his head pondering.

"Son, I think you are right," Rachel said gently. "We will have Paula over so we can explain what transpired here last night and let her make up her own mind. However, son, remember, we are not leaving the church. Not until we have to anyway. We just having Jesus live in our hearts and have dominion over our home. I think Robert and Ruthie would be helpful in this matter. They have been practicing Christians for years and know the Bible inside and out." Rachael stated.

"Let's all pray about it today and have Paula over this evening. Not letting her know would be wrong. I am proud of you son. I also need to let her know about my illness and that I would love nothing more than to have her as my daughter-in-law. She is such a sweet, spirited young woman, I am sure she will understand. Paula's warmness emanates love. It flows from her so easily."

"That sounds wunderbaar gut to me Mamm." Lucas hugged her very carefully; he felt if he hugged her very hard, he might break her. He felt bad he hadn't been giving her more hugs of late; he might have noticed how frail she had been getting.

"Rachael, your eggs and toast are here on the table for you," Sarah offered,. "Would you like some orange juice to go with that?"

Rachael thought how good it sounded, but then she thought of the acid and her system. "It sounds gut, mamm, however, this morning, I believe I will skip the orange juice. Denki for asking though," Rachael said as she seated herself at the table to eat her breakfast.

It wasn't but a few minutes until Jonas rode into the barn. He had to walk the horse to cool her down and then gave her a good brushing. He checked her feet for rocks, put some hay in her stall with half a can of oats and filled her water pail. He gave her a good pat, telling Babe she had been a gut girl.

As he strolled into the house, his mamm called for him to come tell her everything that the ladies had said. After he had conveyed what both Rebeka and Martha had sent him back with, he asked how she felt. He noticed the fancy new furniture item in their living room. It couldn't have been more beautiful, especially compared to what pieces they already owned.

His mamm watched his eyes going over the new daybed. "Jonas, this daybed started out to be a twin bed most likely for the Englischers or a Mennonite family that allows fancier items in their homes."

The back of the daybed was to fit a headboard for a full or queen bed. She explained to him it would not be theirs for the keeping, only a loan. She told him Robert wouldn't take any money for it, so it would be going back.

"It really is too fancy for our home. Don'tcha think?" Rachael asked, taking his hand in hers and looking straight into his hazel eyes. Those eyes showed a strong look of concern.

"Do you have any other messages from the ladies?" Rachael asked.

"Jah Mamm, they both said they would be here about ten this morning." Jonas offered as he leaned over to kiss his Mamm's cheek.

"Ach mei, with my sleeping late, it won't be long before they will be coming up the drive. Allie, will you put on a fresh pot of coffee and put some cookies on a plate? Oh, maybe we should also have plenty of fresh lemonade, cold. I keep forgetting how this weather is already so warm for this time of year. When one sleeps late and hasn't been outside, one forgets about this heat." Rachael finished giving Allie the things she thought needed to be done.

"Rest easy, Mamm, Mammi, Marty, and I have it all redd up and is setting out on the table, and the coffee is brewing," Allie came by to give her mamm a kiss on the her frail cheek.

"Denki gals, you are ever so competent and I should have known better than to even question any of you," Rachael smiled sweetly.

"Jonas, after our family meeting last night, do you have any questions?"

"Not now, Mamm. When we have more time to talk, I do have questions to ask. However, I am headed out to help the men with the planting. We are so close to having it all done. It will give us more time for other projects. Can I get anything for you before going?" Jonas had his arm wrapped around her shoulders. They were so thin and he wondered just how long it had been since he had actually felt her frail body. It is as though she was just skin and bones. He also felt as if she might break. *Lord God, help my mamm, please help with her illness.*

"No, Jonas, you go help your Daed and brooders. I have the girls in here to help if needed." Rachael reached up to give Jonas a hug and a kiss. "Thank you Jonas for delivering my notes to Rebeka and Martha."

"Mamm, please don't hesitate to ask for anything. If I can do it for you, it will be done." Jonas said with a big smile as he left the room. Rachael heard a commotion outside; she knew her menfolk were helping both Martha and Rebeka with their buggies and horses. She realized how blessed she was to have such a loving family and friends.

Rachael got to her feet and went into the kitchen, knowing the two ladies would be coming through the back door as they had for all the years she had known them. Rachael thought back briefly to all these two women had shared with her. They were like sisters. God had blessed her with friends she could count on to help her with anything that might have cropped up over the years. She and Martha had missed Rebeka when Rebeka had gone to Ohio to help her sick sister. Rebeka had been sixteen and had just started her rumschpringe period. They were so glad when she returned and it now seemed that that was a lifetime ago.

"Rebeka, Martha, I'm so pleased you could drop what you were busy with to come at my beckoning. You both know I would not have asked you to come on such short notice if it were not of the utmost importance. I have news, and because we have been lifetime friends, I didn't want you finding out what has happened from anyone else but me."

"Now, let's wipe those frowns from those beautiful faces. Remember, we used to tease each other about frowning and making permanent lines on our faces. We would laugh for hours. Why don't we go into the living room and sit so we can talk in private?" Rachael asked as cheerfully as she could under the circumstances.

Allie stopped by to say her hullos and then left the room.

"I guess it would be best to just tell you both outright and get this suspense over with. I know both of you have plenty of work to attend to, and I would not want to keep either of you from it."

"Rachael, what is it my liewi? You know you can come to either of us for any reason under the sun," Rebeka blurted out.

"I am sick and not going to get any better. I have been told by my doctors that I need to get my things in order. My weight seems to be falling off daily, and I am getting weaker by the day also. I doubt I will be leaving the house from here on out, it tires me to go out too much. The frolic being such a special day with Paula, my upcoming daughter-in-law, I couldn't miss the quilting bee. I may miss their wedding; therefore, I wanted to be in on the quilting bee. Paula will make my Lucas a wunderbaar gut wife."

Martha stood stunned beyond belief, she stuttered, "You are *dying?*"

"Jah, that is what the doctors say. The three of us have been such close friends our whole lives, I knew this news should come from me." Rachael added.

"Rebeka, please tell Laura how grateful we are that she befriended Marty last night. We had a family meeting, and Marty charged out of here before any of us knew she left. Laura found her crying her eyes out. After Laura heard the whole story, she did help Marty to understand that it is not God's fault this is happening and that she should probably get herself home. Laura knew we would be worried sick with her gone. Laura walked Marty home last night. Again, please tell Laura we are very thankful for her thoughtfulness. That is a true friend, just like we have always been."

"Laura walked Marty home last night?" Rebeka's mind racing back and forth from what Laura did, in one hand she wanted to be proud of her, and on the other, she knew Laura disobeyed. But this was not the time to bring Laura into her thoughts. Here her friend needed her, and she wanted to be there for her to the end.

"Jah, she did, however, as I said, I am grateful she walked Marty home. She did not come in. Marty came in to tell us about sharing my illness with Laura. Marty cried, telling us she felt bad for worrying the family. You should be proud of Laura, she said something to Marty to help her understand the situation better than we did and again I am ever so thankful," Rachael stated softly.

"Well, if Laura comforted Marty, I am proud of her. The three of us have been lifetime friends, and we know what it means to have true friendship," Rebeka said. She wanted to get Laura off her mind for now. Rachael's news devastated her.

"Rachael, what did the doctors tell you?" Martha asked gently.

"I have cancer and only weeks to be here with all of you. They have done everything possible, and now I just need my family and friends to share these last few weeks. They are going to mean a lot to everyone involved. My family is already doing what they can to make me comfortable, and I am appreciative. Look at this daybed Robert Miller sent over for me to use. Of course it will go back after my passing. It sure will come in handy now as there are days it is hard to make it upstairs. Now, I want you both to be of good cheer about this. God is in control, and we know that. I have made peace with it, and would like you all to do the same," Rachael said with a big smile. "I don't want sad faces and my family already knows this."

"Rachael, of course we will do whatever it is you want. Is there anything we can do besides just be a friend?" Martha asked.

"Ach mei, just being my friends is exactly what I need. We want to show our families the love we have for one another."

"That sounds gut to me," Rebeka said cheerfully.

Rachael finished telling both ladies about her illness. She kept silent about her new found faith because she didn't feel the timing quite right. She would show them by her walk. She would not willingly put her family at risk and especially at this time. She prayed to God her decisions to leave the Old Order Amish would not place them under the Bann and be shunned.

"I would love to see Lucas and Paula married, but that is a dream I'm sure won't come to pass," Rachael said.

"What if Joseph went to the bishop and got permission? He could take Lucas with him and have a meeting with the brethren and the bishop. They should understand how much a mamm wants to see at least one child married, especially her eldest," Rebeka said.

"That is such a gut idea. I don't know why we hadn't thought of that before. Denki Rebeka," Rachael said with tears of joy on her face.

"We will do whatever it takes to help your family. And if Joseph wants Abe to go with them to see the rest of the brethren and the bishop, I am sure he would be glad to. You don't have a problem with me sharing with Abe what we talked about today, do you Rachael?" Rebeka asked as she got herself redd up to go.

"Let me first tell both Joseph and Lucas your idea. Lucas and Paula are going to be here together this evening so we can share my illness with her. I am sure they would both love to be married as soon as possible, so they will be thrilled at the thought it might come about this soon. I will leave it in God's hands. I will be praying this afternoon, waiting for the menfolk to come in from the field. I understand they should be through today with the last of the planting. That in its self will be a blessing."

"I thank both of you for coming today. Mostly, I thank you for being my best friends all these years. Our daughters will not understand the true meaning of this kind of friendship until they are older and have to lean not only on God but also on their friends. We must always show that love of true friendship so they can see it. I feel blessed having the people in my life as I do. God has been so good to me."

"Rachael, you need not thank either of us. We will be sad not to have you here. We both will be looking in on your girls. I know Sarah is here to help them; she is the best mamm ever, not to mention she is my brooder's mother-in-law. Rest assured, the girls will always know they can come to either of us for anything. We know Sarah is close to both of your girls, but sometimes, it is a woman their mamm's age that they need to talk to," Martha said.

Rachael didn't want to share any more with her friends about Christ just yet so she let it go. Thinking to herself how close her mamm and the girls really were, not to mention how Christ Himself is now in their lives, eased her sense of being. Rachael walked the ladies to the back door and gave them both hugs.

"Please stop by whenever you get a chance. You will not be disturbing me no matter what time it is. With my time being so short, I will have a long time to sleep. So, wipe those worried looks off your faces, it is not allowed in this house." Rachael had a cheerful glow about her.

The ladies hugged her back and made their way out the backdoor. Allie had run out a few minutes earlier to let the menfolk know to get the ladies' horses and buggies redd up. When the ladies reached the end of the walk to the house their buggies stood ready and waiting.

As Rachael made her way back into the living room to lie down on the daybed, her family came in to see what they could get for her. "Please don't fuss so much. I promise to ask if I need something. We are going to run this household as if I am not sick. That may be hard to do; however, I believe you will see things run more smoothly that way. Is that alright with all of you?"

"Right now I am going to lie down on this beautiful daybed with the most exquisite quilt I have seen in a while. I do need to rest for a while. Get back to work with you all!" Rachael said laughing and pretending she had a whip in her hand. The others laughed with her.

Rachael sat in the living room praying to God for wisdom and strength to be of more help to her family. She saw the need in Jonas' face for the talk this evening. *Joseph and I should spend some time in prayer before we start with our family devotional and then our reading in the Gospel of John. We need to put God at the top of everything we do, as God will then be there for them, as it tells us in the Bible, 'I will never leave you nor forsake you.'* This is one of the passages she clung to, it gave her such peace.

Rachael knew she could count on her dear friends. Even though their visit had been so short, it was everything she needed to let her two friends know for now. The entire community would know within the next few days. She felt better after sharing with them; their closeness stretched back for years. She didn't feel ashamed of her new faith; she needed more time with her family, then she would tell them. With their Old Order ways being so rigid in their beliefs; she didn't want them to interfere with her whole family. *This is something the Lord will have to help her work on and through.*

"Mamm, did you have a gut visit with Rebeka and Martha?" Marty asked shyly, not wanting to disturb her mamm if she was resting.

"Ach, we had a real nice visit. I told Rebeka how grateful we were to Laura for talking with you and walking you home. She seemed to be a little disturbed by Laura coming here with you. That is just not like her. Is Laura doing alright?" Rachael asked Marty cautiously.

"Jah, as far as I know she is doing alright. We didn't talk about anything going on in her life. I guess she felt I had enough to deal with; if she did have something she needed to share, she kept it to herself. But remember Mamm, she just turned sixteen and her rumschpringe period will start now, however, she didn't say anything about it." Marty added.

"I believe with her still being in school, her rumschpringe does not start this soon. But school will be out before we know it, and I am so glad. We need you to be at home with us. Your teacher will be bringing your work that needs to be done and to see what is going on. I believe we will have to tell her of my illness. Before she comes, we have something else to discuss with you. Your daed and I will have some time to talk to you this afternoon when he comes in from the fields." Rachael committed looking outside at the sun to see where it sat in the sky.

"What is it Mamm, is it more about your illness?" Marty wanted to know.

"No my liewi, and I don't want to go into it until your daed comes in. Not unless your daed tells me too, I know they are busy trying to finish up. Please don't pester any of the others either."

"Yes, Mamm," Marty said with her head down looking very humble. She knew she should not have run out last night. She now understood it had been harder on her family than she first thought. She wondered what on earth the topic of conversation had been after she left. She stood and excused herself.

She should not have been so hard on her, Rachael thought to herself. However, she knew Marty would have gone around hounding everyone until she would have had them wanting to wrap a kerchief around her mouth to keep her still. Rachael laughed, in Marty's inquisitive thirteen years; there had been many times she had wanted to do that herself. Marty had more questions than all the rest of her kinner put together. She smiled, even though God made each child different, Marty was the one with a million and one questions. However, it would be hers and Joseph's responsibility to tell Marty about Christ in a way she could understand and still keep it to herself. She wasn't a disobedient child, just a chatterbox. The important thing she needed Marty to understand would be the problems the family would experience if she spilled the beans.

The day seemed long with nothing to do. All Rachael could do was to stay out of the way, there were many chores to get done, and she had always done more than her share. Maybe it was going to be hard on the others to pick up the extra work, but for her not being able to help would be even harder. The many adjustments all of them would have to make had to be turned over to God. She said a silent prayer and closed her eyes for a moment.

Just then, in walked the men for lunch, which was ready and waiting for them. They were all big eaters and it made her feel better in one way, knowing they would be alright without her made her feel better in one way but useless in another. That is the flesh part of her getting in the way of what God had for her; she could feel something coming from Him, but what? If she learned to wait on the Lord, He would show her. She needed to learn how to have patience.

Joseph seated himself at the head of the table, and since everyone was already there waiting for him, except Lucas, he began the prayer out loud. Marty looked at both parents.

What's this, another prayer out loud? Daed had said it out loud last night too, darn me for running out. It's my own fault for being so childish about it. Seemed everyone else felt comfortable with it.

"Where is Lucas?" Rachael wanted to know.

"I believe he went to see if Paula would come over this evening to join us for our devotional, Lucas wanted her to be here," Joseph smiled.

The talk around the table became a light conversation. Lunch went by quickly, and before Joseph left the house, Rachael asked if they should speak to Marty together and Joseph told her she would do just fine by herself. Joseph mentioned they were trying to finish with the field work before the heat of the day really hit them.

Rachael and Marty excused themselves after the lunch dishes were washed, dried and the kitchen made redd up for the evening meal.

Rachael sat where she could look into Marty's eyes. She wanted to be able to see her reactions. She thought maybe she could stop and explain when looks of confusion set Marty's jaw tight, that being one of the traits that always gave Marty away.

"Marty, we told the other family members last night about our own new relationship with Jesus. Now, wait and hear me out before getting that look on your face," Rachael stated.

"Mamm, what new relationship with Jesus are you talking about? I know that the prayers have been said aloud several times of late, and I didn't understand that. Can we start there, about the prayers? What is happening?" Marty questioned.

"If you will calm yourself down," Rachael paused, "first of all, sit down. You need not take a tone with me." Rachael said. "I asked you to let me explain, are you going to do that now?"

"I am sorry Mamm," Marty's face dropped and tears were ready to spill down her cheeks. "I think your illness has me on the defensive, and being angry is my way of guarding my heart. I know this is not the way I am supposed to act. Please forgive me, I'll listen."

"I have been studying the Bible and have come to know that without Christ in my heart, and Him being my Lord and Savior, I have no way of going to heaven. Jesus tells us in the Bible that, 'None shall come to the Father except through Me.' That means we must come to know that Jesus is the Son of God, that He died for our sins, and that He rose in three days to show us we can have eternal life by repenting of our sins and asking Him to come live in our hearts," Rachael said softly.

"I have been going to Cousin Ruthie's place to clean a couple times a week, and she knows how sick I really am, therefore, we studied the Bible instead of my working. She paid me as though I worked so no one would be the wiser. We were not trying to deceive anyone, I just needed more time to prepare and share with my family all I had learned. I am what we call a baby Christian. I didn't know enough to share with you for quite some time. The first person I told was your daed. It took him a few days himself to read with me and see why it is so important for me to have Jesus as Lord and Savior." Rachael sighed, stopping to take a drink of water. *This is harder than she thought it would be.*

"Mamm, are you all right?" Marty questioned.

"Jah, I just needed to wet my whistle. Your daed also gave himself to Christ and asked Him to come live in his heart. That is a big change for your daed to make. We have always lived Old Order Amish, and we know we will go under the Bann once this gets outside our house. We are asking all our family members, and this will include Paula, not to say anything that goes on here at home. Please Marty, it may be hard at times to do this, however, the rewards we will receive will make it all worthwhile. It truly is of the utmost importance to your daed right now." Rachael hugged her and kissed her smooth cheek.

"I have a few verses picked out for us to read together. This will help you to understand why I believe the way I do." Rachael read John 3:16 and several verses in the book of Romans. "This is part of the Romans' road to salvation. Marty, this is considered arrogant in the Amish faith. However, the Bible tells us how we get the free gift of salvation from God is through His grace. I want to pray about what we talked about, and you may go to your daed or your mammi if you have questions while I am sleeping. One thing I want you to remember, if I am down here on the daybed you may wake me. I will be here for you." Rachael stated with a grin. "That is, until Jesus comes for me."

Marty looked at her mamm and wondered how they would live like this. With the whole community finding out she knew even at her young age what would happen to those in her family that had joined church. She trusted her parents and knew she must do the reading her mamm had given her, but she also knew of all the praying needed to see them through. She could see the glow of happiness in her mamm's eyes. This assured her there must be something to this newfound faith. She knew her mamm well and could see the pain on her mamm's face, however, when she spoke of God and His Son, her face lit up like sunshine. Radiant being a better word when her mamm spoke of Jesus.

As Marty went up to her room, she hoped to find it empty so she could read the Gospel of John. *Why hadn't their bishop taught them what one must do in order to have salvation? It was as if the bishop had blinders on, not being able to use all of God's Word. The verses are so important to one's own soul, as my mamm just shared with me.*

She felt her parents knew what was best for her, so she wanted to get started. She wanted to read as much as she could in her free time. *Maybe Mamm will read with me after chores are done each day.* Marty was deep in thought and startled when Allie opened the door.

Allie went to the bed and sat beside Marty. She reached for Marty's hand and Marty through herself into her sister arms.

"Marty, we need not only to trust in our parents' wisdom and judgment but also in God and His Son, our Lord and Savior. Please try to be strong for our mamm. It will be so much easier on her if she knows we doing as they ask of us."

"I will Allie, I am just having a hard time knowing we are losing mamm."

Allie cradled her sister for a few moments. *Thank You Father for helping me to help my sister. Please give me the wisdom I need to comfort her. Amen.*

∞

Chapter 15

The Millers were closing up shop; it seemed to be a long day. Uncle Robert decided to stop off to see Joseph and Rachael. He wanted to know if the daybed had worked out for them. It was not something he normally made, and at best, he felt it a makeshift daybed. If it worked for them, he would feel good about giving it to them.

He couldn't get Rachael off his mind all day and he really wanted to check in on her. She had always been such a hard worker and a wonderful person. He knew Joseph would be lost when she passed on and Joseph had not gone into any detail. That had left him with a feeling it must be a pretty serious matter. Especially for them to want a piece of furniture to go in the living room for Rachael to lie on during the day.

Jacob wanted to go with him, but Micah wanted to get home, get his chores done, and be off to see his sweetheart. As for Jacob, he hoped it would take a while before he would be looking for a sweetheart, but Uncle Robert was not aware his eyes were already on Laura.

"Hullo," Robert said as he climbed down from the wagon. "Would it be all right with you if we stopped in to see Rachael for a few minutes?"

"Jah, she is resting on the daybed you fixed up for us, and it is just what she needed," Joseph said nodding at Robert showing his appreciation.

"Uncle Robert, I don't know her well, however, Rachael's always been so nice to me I would like to say hullo to her. Would that be all right?" Jacob inquired.

"She would have it no other way young man. Go on in. Say, didn't I see you at Laura's birthday party?" Joseph asked.

"Jah sir, you did. I haven't been here too long and my cousin, Micah, wanted me to go. Both of us are from Ohio and our parents still live there. My mamm is Uncle Robert's sister. It sure is nice here and I hope to be here for a long while. Uncle Robert's been gut to show me much in the woodworking business. I guess it runs in my veins as well as in Micah's and Uncle Robert's."

As they made their way into the living room the ladies saw them coming and brought refreshments. They thought after working with the dust in the furniture shop all day, the two would like some ice tea or lemonade.

"Ach mei, how wunderbaar gut it is to see you both," Rachael said. "Is Lisa with you?"

"No, she is at home. We just stopped by on our way home. I wanted to make sure there isn't something else we might do," Robert said.

"Denki for asking, however, this is plenty. I want you to know, it will be in the same condition when you get it back. We love it, but we think it a bit too fancy for our house," Rachael said laughingly, "I do hope you will let Lisa know she is welcome anytime she can get away." Rachael's smile lit up the room until it almost glowed. Her eyes were sparkling with excitement.

She wanted lots of company, how else was she to be that shining light for Jesus. *Lord, please help me with words to share with them.* She asked the Lord for wisdom. She needed to follow her own advice, let go and let God. Why is that so hard to do when it affects us personally?

"We didn't come to stay long or to tire you out Rachael, so we will be on our way. I'll tell Lisa what you said about stopping by. She will be glad to help in any way she can, just let her know." Robert came to take Rachael's hand in his and as he did so, he saw a real peace about her. He didn't see any fear in her whatsoever, *what a strong faith God has given her,* he thought. He hoped that when his day came, he could also show that strength and peace in himself.

"Let's get home Jacob, Lisa will be wondering what happened to us," Robert said, patting Jacob on his back in a fatherly manner.

After they left and headed down the road Jacob couldn't help but asked his Uncle about what was on his mind, "Uncle Robert, for a person being so sick, Rachael doesn't appear to be in any pain. Did you see the peace upon her face and in her eyes? Yes, she has lost weight, but since coming here, Rachael's always been so perky in spirit and so nice. It is hard to find the right words to explain what feelings she portrayed. We all know God does work miracles. Maybe Rachael is one of His miracles. I hope I am not speaking out of turn." Jacob said and sat quietly waiting for Uncle Robert to answer.

Robert, also deep in thought, had seen everything Jacob had and more. The Beachy Amish from Ohio lived their lives as Rachael did. They are a little more modern, but held to the Old Order as much as possible. Robert's own family members lived Beachy Amish, most of which didn't join the church, therefore; no one in his immediate family was Banned from the community. They all went around as though it were a daily party they were attending. Not so much as getting away from the Old Order; they were just happier with lighter attitudes and with a love that glowed in most of them for each other. He decided to share with Lisa that evening, and maybe she could shed some light on what he had missed. He felt a warming in his heart and sheer delight to see Rachael looking that peaceful. He prayed and thanked God for His mercy and grace. He also thought about what they had done there after receiving the letter from their bishop; he wondered if joining the Old Order Amish church had been a wise decision.

He struggled with that, and he and Lisa talked it over until they decided since there were no Beachy Amish there, they would join the Old Order. He prayed to God they had done the right thing. They kept their praying to Jesus to themselves, but would not change their minds about their beloved Lord and Savior.

"Jacob, it was very nice of you to want to see her. Most young folks have a hard time dealing with sickness. I thought maybe it was an excuse to see Allie. She is a very pretty young lady. She has stayed at home to help her mamm and family since she quit school two years ago. I haven't even heard of her being out to the singings. However, I could see you were actually there to see Rachael for yourself. It shows me what an unselfish person you are. Caring for others is so important in this life, and I am proud of you. I am also proud of the work you have been doing. Keeping up with Micah will give you something to strive for. He can teach you a lot. He has almost surpassed me in some areas. Watch and learn, son," Robert said as they were going up their drive to the house.

Jacob kept his feelings to himself. He only had eyes for Laura ever since the first time he had met her. He thought that her falling right into his arms had to be some kind of a sign from God. Jacob pondered the situation a moment. He would wait on the Lord and his best friend, Jesus, before getting carried away. All Jacob knew for sure and for certain was that God was so good to him.

∞

Chapter 16

Lucas had been praying throughout the day. The only thing he knew for sure and for certain is was that he would stick with his folks in their beliefs. He couldn't remember not having a close relationship with his family, and if he and Paula had joined the church, they also would be put under the Bann. He knew now he could not go through with that plan, he only prayed that Paula would want to join them. He knew what his folks and grandparents were in for ….the Bann.

He wanted to walk over to see Robert and Ruthie. With his family always being close with them as they were not under any Bann, he felt he could ask Robert most anything. He needed to find out for himself if Robert actually thought he was saved. The word *saved* was what he was having a problem with. They knew about Jesus Christ being the Son of God, but that wasn't talked about among the Old Order Amish. It was almost noon, supper time, and Lucas thought he would ride over to the Lapp house and talk to them now. He knew he would be missing the main meal of the day.

Just as Lucas arrived, Robert got out of his car. Lucas thought the car was something special, but had never thought until now about having one of his own someday.

"Robert, can you spare me a few minutes of your time?" Lucas asked.

"Why, of course Lucas," Robert said, "What is on your mind? It is not like you to take yourself away from your work in the middle of the day. Is it your mamm?" Robert questioned with a look of concern.

"Yes and no. I know that sounds odd, however, Mamm told us about her being saved, that Jesus had died for our sins, and that it was all right for us to say we are saved, that is, if we ask forgiveness and repent. I am not sure it says it in the Bible; however, the Amish have never been allowed to say that regardless. We are to wait for Judgment Day and see if we are in favor with God." Lucas wondered.

"We want to believe in the whole Bible, don't we?" Robert said kindly. Robert didn't want to start off by offending Lucas. He knew it was going to be difficult for some of Rachael's family members to accept. He waited for Lucas to think about what he had said.

"Yes, I do want to believe all of God's Word. It is just so hard to understand why the Old Order kept us from reading the whole Bible. Why would they do that?"

"There are a lot of questions I do not have answers to, and that is one of them. I can go over things in the Bible with you; however, I only know what God tells us to do. He tells us that if we believe Jesus is His Son, and confess our sins with our mouth, ask Jesus into our hearts to live, and turn from our sins, we will have our names placed in the Book of Life. This is where we would find we are saved by grace and not by works. In Ephesians 2:8-9 tells us, 'For by grace you have been saved through faith, and that not of yourselves, it is the gift of God, not of works, lest anyone should boast' We are to go forth and tell the Good News of Jesus Christ. I am going to do what the Bible tells me to do. How about you? Have you read the parts in the Bible your mamm asked you to read?" Robert asked.

"Jah, I did read some of them. Paula and I were to start instruction at our church soon. I need to get over to talk to Paula and then get back to work. Thank you, Cousin Robert, for taking some time to talk with me. I know I have a lot to learn, and I need to make a decision soon. I need to know if Paula will still marry me if I want to follow my parents. I don't know how to bring all of this up to her," Lucas said, rubbing his chin.

"Why don't you pray about it? Let the Lord lead you, Lucas," Robert said, "and your mamm would tell you to follow God, not man."

"Jah, you are right about that. I think I will ask Paula to come over to our place this evening, I am sure of our love. Now, learning to let the Lord lead in all things, that is going to take some time and lots of prayers," Lucas said.

"Ruthie and I will keep you in our prayers as we have been with your mamm, actually, your whole family. 'Trust in the Lord with all your heart, and lean not unto your own understanding'," Robert said as Lucas made his way down the drive.

"I remember that verse," Lucas said. "Proverbs, right?"

Robert smiled, "Jah, look it up and read all of chapter three. It makes more sense every time I read it. We must learn to trust in the Lord without giving it a second thought. It is about letting God be in control. Let go and let God."

"Thanks again," Lucas said and hurried off to visit with Paula and get back before the supper hour was over. His stomach told him it would be a long time until dinner.

As Lucas knocked on the back door of the Miller house, Paula greeted him with a look of surprise, "Is it your mamm?" Paula's concerned expression was written all over her pretty face. Lucas pulled her close and just held her for a few moments.

"Not like you think," Lucas said. "I came by to see if you could come over and talk with me and my family this evening." Lucas stated.

"Why sure, my liewi, should I come now? I would if your mamm needed the help, you know." Paula wanted to know. "If not, I should be able to be there right after helping here with the dinner dishes. I am sure the Millers would not mind if it is urgent." Paula said with worry lines on her forehead. She knew her Aunt Lisa would understand; she had become almost as close to her as her own mamm. She had been blessed her Uncle Robert had married such a gut wife. Lisa is so kind to all she meets.

"No, after dinner will be just fine. And I can never spend too much time with you. I can't wait to make you my wife. However, we have some things to discuss with my family after we have some time to ourselves. As a matter of fact, I may need to have my mamm in on our conversation if that is all right with you." Lucas stated.

Paula had a lot of questions; however, she nodded her acceptance. "I'll be over as soon as possible." She could tell Lucas needed to hurry back home to work, but at the same time, she wanted him to have a drink of something cool before he took his leave. "Would you at least have some lemonade or sweet tea before heading out?"

"Just water would be great, you are so kind to ask," Lucas said with a grin at the corners of his mouth. After drinking the water he left saying he would be looking forward to seeing her that evening.

Jonas and John were just finishing up with supper and were heading outside. They didn't know what to think about Lucas since he hadn't been there to eat with them. They didn't remember him ever taking off like this during the day before.

"Jonas, what do you think Lucas is up to?" John asked.

"I am not sure, however, I think we should wait and see if he is here to work with us this afternoon before getting ourselves worked up," Jonas said. He no sooner got those words out of his mouth, and Lucas appeared.

"Brooder, what happened to you at supper?" John asked.

Being the younger of the two boys, John always seemed to be right underfoot. He always felt John needed to know his whereabouts more than he should. Even when Lucas started his rumschpringe period, John would sneak out to where the courting buggy sat parked while not in use and ask Lucas if he could go. Lucas used to laugh at him and send him back to bed. However, John was fifteen, and Lucas thought him too old to be nosing around in other people's business.

"John, why do you believe it is any of your concern? There comes a time when it is not funny or polite. We were not raised like that, and I am to blame for letting you go on acting out like this. From now on, you had better be on your best behavior, as this family is going to go through a lot of changes. We are going to stick together with our folks." Lucas said leading the way out to the barn.

"Jonas and I have been praying this morning and decided the first thing we are too young to make our own decision concerning faith, and second, we also prayed to be as helpful to the family as possible.

We know mamm is counting on us, and we are not going to let her down," John said.

"I am very pleased with the way you boys are looking at the family as a whole. That is exactly what it is going to take to get us through this rough time. Remember boys, none of us will go under the Bann. It will only be our parents and our grandparents. If you later decide, you can always go to the bishop and tell him your decision," Lucas stated. With that said they all headed back to work.

Marty and Allie sat on the bed holding each other. They both knew their mamm wanted them to read the Bible. They got their Bibles and opened to the Gospel of John.

"I think that reading the Bible together will help both of us to understand. When one of us has a question, we can stop and look it up or write down our questions for later, when we meet with the family," Allie stated.

"I am so glad to have such a gut sister," Marty said. "I don't know what I would do without you. I know mammi will be here for us, but it is not the same as being close to you."

They sat for an hour reading the Bible, prayed together and then went downstairs to help prepare the evening meal. They wanted everything done as soon as possible so the family could join around the table for their time of prayer and study.

Paula showed up at just the perfect time. She wanted to do as Lucas had asked her to. The family gathered at the table with their Bibles in hand. The dinner dishes had been cleaned up and everything done before Paula arrived.

Lucas knew the topic of faith and his mamm coming to saving grace should come from her and asked his family to give them a few minutes alone. Lucas took Paula out to the backyard where the swing sat. He invited her to have a seat and looked into those eyes he always seemed to get lost in. "Paula, with Mamm being so sick, would you please let her explain to you what has been going on in our house? Then we can talk later, and you can give me the answer to my question about becoming my wife."

"Of course I will listen to your mamm. What's this question, will I marry you? I thought it almost written in stone! However, my first reaction is the concern I have for your mamm. It is obvious to those of us who care so much about her that her health is a big issue. What is going on with her, Lucas?"

"It is something I would like for her to tell you about. She will explain briefly before we tell you the rest of our family news. Let's go inside so we don't keep them waiting," Lucas suggested.

Paula didn't know how to share what she'd kept to herself all these months. However, she knew it must come out soon. *God, please help me to use wisdom and to do Your will in all ways. Amen.*

As they entered the kitchen they found everyone waiting at the table. Rachael's smile was warm and cheerful as usual. Paula saw nothing but love coming from her future mother-in-law. The family had left two places open for them to sit. "Do you need something to drink?" Rachael questioned.

"No, I will be fine, denki for asking though. I am anxious for you to tell me how you are feeling. Lucas said there has been a new development, is that true Rachael?" Paula wanted to know.

"Well, the doctors have sent me home with bad news, but that led me to find the Good News," Rachael said.

"What do you mean good news? I am sorry to say, but you don't look well, how does good news play into the bad news?"

"I didn't state that very well, did I? They sent me home with news of cancer in my body, and there is nothing they can do about it. However, God can. I learned about Jesus Christ, and He is the Good News," Rachael said.

"I am very confused about what you are trying to tell me. Can you back up to the doctors and the cancer?" Paula asked again.

"I can, however, I gave my life to Jesus and asked Him to come live in my heart. In doing so I also asked forgiveness of my sins. I became a child of God through His grace, and now I am assured of eternity. So to me, this is the best news anyone could ask for. We are here on earth but a short time, and the only way to the Father is through the Son. We need only pray in Jesus Christ's name that God's will be done, not ours. When I gave my life to Jesus, He became my Lord and Savior. Let us pray that the Holy Spirit touches each heart here this evening." Rachael said.

After Joseph led them in prayer, they all looked up to see Paula's face full of questions. She could hardly believe her ears. Paula had struggled with her own newfound faith ever since she arrived on the bus, and not knowing what to do with it, she had kept it to herself. She knew she loved Lucas and wanted to be his wife and would stay in the Amish faith if that was what he wanted. But since her arrival in Lancaster County, she continued praying silently but studied her Bible diligently. She felt compelled to pray out loud and tell of her Savior, however, many eyebrows would have touched the ceiling, and she felt she would have been in trouble.

Paula was shocked with the fact that Rachael, Joseph, and their family had also accepted Jesus. She shook her head, wanting to share with them, but she was afraid she might not have understood exactly what had transpired here. She stopped for a few seconds and prayed to God, silently, for help. She didn't want to trip over her tongue in case she had misconstrued what they were trying to tell her.

"That should not have been the way we started our prayer, it wasn't fair of us to say the prayer out loud before telling you. When the disciples asked Jesus how to pray, He told them they could pray directly to the Father. He also said in John 14:14, 'If you ask anything in My name, I will do it.' John 14:15 says, 'If you love Me, keep my commandments.' So you see Paula, we are only doing what Jesus is telling us to do. We know you and Lucas were to start instruction in the church soon. Now after hearing this about our new faith, you need to let Lucas know if you can follow him. We want you to be a part of this family; however, you need to pray about what God has planned for your life," Rachael encouraged.

Paula fell into Rachael's arms. She cried on her shoulder, not wanting to put much weight on Rachael but needing that motherly touch. She could not believe how the events of this evening were answers to her prayers to God just before she arrived, actually, those had been her prayers for months now.

"My heart has been so heavy ever since I arrived from Ohio. I kept what I learned on my bus ride here to myself, and now I know how wrong that was. This cute little lady I sat by shared God with me about halfway here. She told me there was but one way to the Father. I studied on my own after my arrival, however, I didn't know what to do about my new faith. I felt bad not telling Lucas before. I kept praying for an answer about how to tell Lucas without losing him. I know 'Jesus is the Way the Truth and the Life.' I have been faithful in my prayers, and now I feel they have all been answered." Paula said as tears of joy trickled down her cheeks. "Of course I will marry you and follow you as long as God is made front and center of our home, now and forever."

"Ach Mei! Praise God, Paula! This has been such a worry of mine ever since my parents shared with the family last night. I had to put all my worries in God's hands and let Him go before this. But thank you, my liewi, for accepting Jesus even when you did. You will be a wonderful help to all of us here. Well, maybe not my mamm, but to the rest of us," Lucas said with a huge smile that could not have been wiped off for anything.

Paula smiled back and reached out hugging him. *God is so good*, she thought to herself.

∞

Chapter 17

Rebeka was keeping herself busy in the kitchen when Laura came through the door after school. As Laura looked around she saw her mamm give her a look of disdain. She shook her head and told Laura to go change into her work frock and come back downstairs.

When Rebeka had gotten home from seeing Rachael earlier in the morning, she thought about telling Abe the news she had learned from Rachael about Laura having been at the Lapp's place the previous night. However, she decided she would to talk to Laura first. If it didn't go well, she would then tell Laura her daed would be dealing with her.

It was as though Laura had totally ignored her parents and their rules Rebeka thought. She had become a completely different person lately. She had always been a little testy in her ways, but this new attitude brought out the worst in her. On one hand she was proud of Laura for befriending Marty; however, it would not have taken her long to let her parents know she would be walking Marty home. Rebeka found herself shaking her head. She was baffled as to why one of her children would disobey her that had never disobeyed her before. This was all so new to her.

She couldn't help but be upset with the news of Rachael's illness. She had only shared with Abe so far. He held her out in the barn as she shed tears for her friend when she returned home. Rachael had asked him to be strong for and with her. She had let the tears roll down her cheeks; that had given her some relief of what had built up on the ride home. She had known Rachael her whole life and couldn't imagine life without her. Rachael was their ray of sunshine.

She knew that God was always in control of their lives and that His plans He had for them, were not always to their liking. However, Rachael's friendship all these years is something she would miss terribly. She could never remember not having Rachael in her life. Their families lived close and they were naturally always together.

With Martha and Rachael always being the closest in their age group, she felt they were more like sisters than friends. It would be very hard not having her here with them and she knew Martha must be feeling the same way.

Rebeka thought of the past six months, they knew Rachael started going to the doctor more than a year ago. She wondered how, if Rachael had been this sick all those months, how is it that she had continued working for Ruthie? Again, she found herself shaking her head. "Ach mei!" she said louder than she meant too.

"Mamm, did you say something?" Mary asked.

"I guess I did say that out loud, didn't I? Just thinking about all that happened today, my mind is running on overload. When your daed comes in for the evening, we will tell everyone everything I was told at Rachael's place today." Rebeka said sighing.

Laura changed and went back down to the kitchen. She knew from the look her mamm had given her that she was not to dally. No one knew she had left the property last night except Mary. Surely, Mary would keep her word about not saying anything once she heard the entire story.

"Laura, were you off the property last night?" Rebeka asked with her hands firmly pressed to each hips.

Laura's eyes flashed back to Mary; however, Mary shrugged her shoulders as if to tell Laura she didn't know how their mamm could have found out. "Mamm, why don't I sweep the walk out front and give you and Laura some time together," Mary said.

"That would be gut, denki Mary," Rebeka replied, her eyes still looking straight at Laura. Mary hurried out the door.

"Jah Mamm, I walked Marty home last night. I found her in the field crying her eyes out. We walked for a while and talked. Her mamm is very sick, and Marty felt distraught, so I didn't want her to be alone. I didn't think it wrong to walk her home."

"Did it ever occur to you to come tell your daed and me what you were going to do?" Rebeka asked.

"I guess I didn't think you would mind under the circumstances," Laura said without much thought.

"I didn't tell your daed, I wanted to talk to you first. Your attitude is what I am worried about. You are not out of school yet, and your daed told you just last night that you would not be leaving the property until then, at least not by yourself anyway. Did you not understand what he said?" Rebeka asked sternly.

"Mamm, with Marty being beside herself, I didn't think about myself at all. I am sorry for not coming to let you know I walked her home, truly I am. With her mamm being such a gut friend to you and to our whole family for so many years, I felt her pain. I could not even think of losing you. Please forgive me this one time."

"Well, I will not say anything to your daed at this point, however, if I find you are not sticking to our rules, rest assured, I will tell your daed. I am not pleased with your actions here of late. Sometimes, I wish we had not let you go to school these past two years. You seem to want to be in the world even though you know that is not our way. Think about how you look to the community, it reflects on your whole your family as well as the People. Being Amish we do not behave in that manner. You are taking on a worldly attitude, and Amish do not behave like that. This is not going to go unnoticed. What do we have to do to make ourselves clear?" Rebeka asked.

"Again, I am truly sorry, I will not leave the property except to finish up with school and go with the family, I promise." Laura stated and walked into the living room.

Rebeka stood there watching her daughter leave the kitchen. She stood shaking her head in disbelief that Laura had become such a handful. Ach, she felt very torn about getting after Laura for being a friend to Marty.

Rebeka thought that if that had been the only thing Laura had done, it would be one thing. However, with her already acting out, it is a big concern for her and her husband. All that is being asked of her is to wait until school was out. I don't believe that is asking too much, she thought. She prayed. *Please God, give Abraham and me the wisdom to guide her through this time. We place her in Your hands. Thank You, Father, for keeping her safe. We ask You to watch over her. Please help her make the right decisions for her life.*

Her thoughts turned to Rachael. She must get over to see her as much as possible. Thinking back to when she, Rachael, and Martha were as tight as three peas in a pod, she also knew they would have been there for each other no matter what. With those thoughts tucked into the back of her mind, Rebeka set about preparing the evening meal for her family.

Mary with broom in hand continued sweeping when Laura came out the front door. Laura was obviously mad and thought Mary had betrayed her. But lately Laura had seemed mad about everything lately, to Mary's way of thinking. Mary sure wished she could figure out how to help her, but Mary found it hard to know what to say without setting Laura off on another tangent. She loved her sister dearly no matter what. Mary finished sweeping and headed for the yard to pull weeds, there were always weeds to pull, and if possible she wanted to avoid the wrath of Laura.

Laura watched Mary working in the yard; she hesitated to seek her out for any opinion on the subject. She still didn't know how her mamm could have found out about her having walked Marty home. She decided to ask her sister straight out. "Mary, did you tell Mamm about my being off the property last night?" Laura questioned.

"Ach mei Laura, I would never do that to you. I didn't want to get you in any trouble. You should not have been out like that, but that is your business. You looked so happy to be with Jacob, why would I spoil your time with him? Besides, you weren't doing anything as far as I could tell that would bring question to you. So long as you behave according to Amish doctrine and God's laws, I saw no reason to say anything to anyone. I know I am not perfect, so why would I go out of my way to snitch on you? Laura, I love you dearly, little sister. We have always been close, well, that is until Micah came into the picture.

"I want that for you when you find your special person, and you will know when it happens. I know you are going through some changes right now, but out of respect for our parents and our Amish faith, we must be careful about how we present ourselves to the Englischers world. I know you are excited to begin your rumschpringe as soon as school is out, but you can't be running around the way you have been.

"Can you give our parents these few days they asked for? Then you and Abby will be going to the singings. I wouldn't let myself be caught out again, I don't want to see you in trouble. Deep down I know you are a gut sister, and I am proud of you. If you feel you have questions about the rumschpringe, please come talk to me." Mary hugged her and the two of them headed off to complete some chores and help finish up with dinner.

"Maybe I am just a little bit out of control," Laura said. "I'm not sure why I thought I already had free rein. Truth be known, I think I am so desperate to be a part of the Englischer world that I got ahead of myself. I get so caught up with my own feelings and desires that I forget how I am to behave. The People want to try and make me be this perfect person, but I am not. I want to make my own mistakes, learn from them, and to do whatever I want to. I thought we were not to be criticized for trying our wings in the Englischer world. What if I do want to leave the Amish faith and go into the Englischers world? What is so wrong with that? Maybe being Amish is not for me," Laura said with that defensive tone in her voice again.

"Ach mei, Laura! There you go again, being defensive with me when you have no need to be. You could not have shocked me more with your statement about going worldly, though," Mary said with sadness in her voice, letting Laura know she would hate to lose her to the world.

"Ach, but you misunderstand, I did not say I was going to leave the Amish faith. I just want the choice, isn't that why we have the rumschpringe period? Isn't that the whole point of it? To see what it is like out in the world so we won't feel like we've been deprived of something? Then later in life, we can look back and be happy for the life we have or hope we don't regret the choices we made. That is the only reason I want to know everything there is to know about the outside world." Laura said with her eyes dancing with much excitement. She found it hard to explain herself, even to her sister.

"Please be careful, it would break our parents' hearts to lose you to the world," Mary said.

"How can we make good decisions without proper knowledge of the unknown? I want to sow my wild oats, as they say, before I have to make my choices. I have longed for this period of my life since your rumschpringe started, it is a very strong yearning in me, and I need to follow my heart right now. I can't explain it any better. I'm sorry if I hurt anyone, I truly don't mean to. We get these mixed signals from the adults. 'Go have fun; just don't do anything that might go against our beliefs.' We do things that otherwise would be forbidden during that time?" Laura explained in exasperation.

"You do make a good case, Laura. It does help me to understand you a little better. I don't agree completely with you, but at least I understand what you're feeling. I will try to be more patient when things arise and not be so judgmental.

"Laura, I miss our little talks and the closeness we shared. I know we may have not thought so at the time, but when we were younger, our lives were a lot less complicated. Let's try to stay close and not let any bitterness come between us. I love you sister," Mary said with deep love in her voice that had been missing for a while.

"Ach Mary, I love you too. I do wish things could be less complicated. I also miss the closeness we used to share, but life goes on, we grow up. We can work on a new relationship as adults, and I will do my best not to be bitter toward you or anyone else." Laura stated as she hugged her sister in return.

∞

Chapter 18

As Lucas helped Paula down from his courting buggy, he could still not wipe the grin off his face. Jah, he wished she had been honest from the start; however, he didn't know how he would have reacted before this time in his life. And the one thing he knew for sure and for certain is that he loved her.

"Ach Paula, I can't believe you kept all you knew about Jesus inside all this time. Will you please promise me one thing before we marry, you won't keep anything as important as this secret from me ever again? We can't have a solid marriage if we hide things from each other," Lucas said softly. He loved her more than he could possibly fathom.

"I am so sorry and I realize it was wrong. Please forgive me for being so foolish. I do promise to never keep anything from you ever again, no matter how I think you might react to it. Can you forgive me?" Paula asked.

"Of course I forgive you," Lucas said. "Now, that leads me to another question. Will you marry me this summer? I want to give you enough time, but it can't be soon enough for me. Now that we are not going to go through with the Amish wedding or their traditions, why wait?" Lucas wanted to know.

"Why wait indeed? Why do we have to wait until summer? I could be a lot of help to your mamm, and I could also lighten the burden of the household chores so the girls can spend more time with her. That is more important to me than waiting to redd up things for a large wedding. I know we are still young, but in past generations, they married earlier than they do now. So what do you say?" Paula was so excited.

Lucas saw the gleam in her eyes and thought, *She is so precious to me, why would we wait? Waiting makes no sense to either of us.* "Let me talk this over with my parents. I am all in favor of it. And I do believe you are right about being a big help to the womenfolk in our house. I want you to know, though, that for the time being, we are going to keep this within our immediate family. We don't want Mamm Banned from the community let alone from her lifelong friends. The doctors are telling her she doesn't have much time left, and a shunning is a hard thing to go through. Her health is fragile at this point and I don't believe she could go through it. She needs her friends' right up to the end. That is such a hard thing for me to imagine her not being here with us. She has been the best mamm anyone could want. Do you understand that I only want her end days to be happy ones?" Lucas asked.

"I do understand you want to protect your mamm from the Bann," Paula said. "It is not something I would wish for anyone to go through, especially not when they are as sick as your mamm is. You can rest assured my lips are sealed. I am sorry to say they have been sealed to protect my own hide up until this evening. I just knew that I loved you so much that I could not think about telling someone for fear you would have nothing to do with me. I know now how wrong I was not to trust in the Lord.

"Your mamm is right; we are to go forth with the Good News about Christ. I need to ask God's forgiveness as fear is also a sin. And not telling you was another sin. I guess most of my night will be spent on my face before God," Paula said with a sadness Lucas had never seen on her face before.

"Paula, I believe you have already asked God to forgive you by confessing to my family tonight about all of it," Lucas said, trying to take the pain away he saw in her face. *She is so pretty! She should not be wearing a frown.*

"I am going to say gut night and let you get back to your family. I believe they were going to study for a while longer, and maybe you can get in on the last of it. I know how important it is going to be to your mamm that her children understand God's Word, and there is a lot to understand. Even with my reading the Bible for the past two years, I still have many questions to ask someone who has had more training in God's Word," Paula said softly.

"Jah, I do believe I will get myself home in hopes I can be with the family. Gut night, and I will discuss with my folks about our plans to go ahead and marry. I don't think they will have a problem with it. I for one would sure be sad not to have my mamm with us on our wedding day. I do remember my daed saying he didn't want to bring anything out into the open as he didn't want Mamm under any unnecessary stress. So I am not sure how this will work. However, my liewi, we will somehow make this happen. We will put all our faith before God and let it rest in His hands." Lucas kissed her on the cheek and took his leave.

Paula hollered softly her goodbye. "Remember Lucas, if God is for us, who can be against us." Lucas entered the kitchen to find his family all laughing and being silly. With his mamm being so sick he couldn't help but wonder where she drew her strength from. "Mamm, you seem to be feeling better. Are you?" Lucas asked.

"Ach Lucas, we were laughing with Marty and her being so serious. We are not going to be serious in this house except when we are praying or studying God's Word. That is the only time I will tolerate seriousness. However, we were not scolding her, just loving her. And as I said the laughter was not at her, but with her. Come join us. We just finished more in the Gospel of John 7:30. 'Therefore they sought to take Him; but no one laid a hand on Him; because His hour had not yet come.' So, you see, God is in control of everything in our lives as He always has been," Rachael shared with her eldest son. "After we wrap things up here why don't we have that private chat you wanted?"

"I would love to join you, denki for asking me. I have some things to share. Paula and I discussed some things I need your approval on, would that be all right" Lucas asked.

"Sure son, we would be more than happy to hear what is on your mind," Joseph said lightly.

Lucas noticed a big change in his daed. The love he saw between his parents was a sheer delight. Lucas pondered; *Marriage is until death do we part. How can my daed be so happy?*

"Children, how about some dessert before you all turn in for the night?" Mammi asked.

"I don't know what we would do without you, Sarah," Joseph replied. He loved his wife's mamm as much as he did his own. The wonderful, sweet spirit of joy that came from God emanated from her.

"We are all in this for the duration," Sarah replied. 'All,' God tells us in the Bible, is 'all.' He wants us to love one another and help one another always, not just in a time of need. There is no reason to thank me for helping my daughter or any of you for that matter. I love each and every one of you. I want you to know that I am pleased with the way the family chose to stay together in the faith. We can keep it here under this roof for the time being," Sarah added, "but it won't be long before it does get out. We must be strong and never be ashamed of loving Jesus."

The family enjoyed dessert; the smacking of their lips in satisfaction and burping showing their appreciation of how good it was. Once the dishes were carried to the sink, Rachael and Joseph ordered the younger ones off to bed.

"I know you are dying to tell us of your plans, and we are dying to hear them," Rachael said to Lucas. "Why don't you go ahead and start?"

"Paula and I want to go ahead with our wedding since we are not going to join church. We know we are young; however, Paula wants to move in so she can be of help to Mamm and Mammi. That would free up some time for the girls to spend with you also. She is so full of love and joy in her heart that it can only be coming from God. She promised she would never keep anything from me again. The only thing we are worried about is how our marriage would affect our situation here at home. We do not want Mamm going under the Bann, but we want her to be there with us on our special day. Do you think we can work something out?" Lucas asked with a look of concern.

"One thing is for sure and for certain, it would put us under the Bann. However, I also want to be there for your wedding, and I believe

God will give me the strength to deal with the Bann if that is what happens. Let's pray about it, then let go and let God. We will put this in His hands, and no matter what, we will have not only Him, but we will have our family together. Remember, we are not alone in this. We have Robert and Ruthie to help us and to fellowship with. I am sure there will be others too as God knows our hearts. He says, 'He will never leave us nor forsake us. He will never give us more than we can bear'," Rachael said. As some were going to speak, she held up her hand for a moment of silence.

"What do you say we start planning the wedding? I do want to be there," Rachael's face was glowing with joy, "we have a lot to do. Is Paula sure she will forgo the big wedding she had planned on?"

"Ach mei, jah! She will be so excited about your approval of an earlier wedding I can barely contain myself from going back over there to tell her." Lucas laughed, but the tears did show to his Mamm. She couldn't help but think they were tears of joy.

"What is she going to tell the Miller family? Does she have any idea how she would deal with that? I know some of the Millers in Ohio have been Beachy Amish for years. There were a few that went along with the split and, they are now Mennonite. So she must have been through some of this before," Joseph said.

"Her family is Beachy Amish. Some of her cousins who never joined church are Mennonites. She said she has always been close to her cousins. She even writes to them now, so I am sure her family won't be too shocked. The best thing that happened is that we didn't start instruction. So, we won't go under the Bann. What I am worried about is the fact that you, Daed, and Mammi and Daadi will go under the Bann. What of your lifelong friends, Rebeka and Martha? Do you think they will stick to the law of the church and not see you, Mamm? I know how much that would hurt you." Lucas voiced concerns for his mamm's feelings.

"Let's not dwell on that," Rachel responded. "We will take one day at a time. Besides, God tells us not to look to man or woman because they will always let us down. We are to look to God for everything."

"We are still going to live the same way we always have," Joseph stated. "Not much will change there. We will still tend our land and try to stay in amongst the People," Joseph offered his opinion.

"How about we get ourselves off to bed after a family prayer?" Joseph said.

Several days went by and Rachael invited both Martha and Rebeka to come back over for another visit. She knew she needed to explain how she had accepted Jesus as her Lord and Savior, and she prayed to God to help her friends understand. The morning chores were done, and the bread making was in progress. The smell of rising bread dough when it hit your nostrils made her stomach growl, a smell no one could misplace. Rachael inhaled and sighed praying she might have a small piece before it hurt her stomach. She then gave God thanks for all He did for her. It was as though she could feel His arms around her, she smiled.

Rebeka and Martha had sent word they would be over this morning. Before Joseph left to tend the chores outside, she asked him to pray with her that both of her dear friends would hear her out. She knew in her heart of hearts she couldn't have gotten through this time alone if her beloved husband had not accepted Christ. He had changed so much since that first night she had shared everything with him, and so she knew he would understand how hard this conversation would be for her. She looked at the time and knew they would be here soon.

It wasn't long and Rachael heard the buggies coming up the lane with Martha in the lead. Joseph and the boys were there to help the ladies out and take their horses to the shady side of the barn. Rachael sighed with thanksgiving for the many blessings she had with all of her family. Now to just speak with her two best friends and she prayed they would listen with open hearts. *God, please help me show them Your love through this illness. Please give me the wisdom and right wording.*

"Ach mei, how wunderbaar gut it is to see you up and looking so gut this morning," Martha stated as the two entered the kitchen.

"You do look better, and that glow about you doesn't fit with your being so sick. I wonder if maybe the doctors were wrong," Rebeka stated.

"First, sit with me so we can catch up on our families for a few minutes, and then I will get into what I need to talk to you about before you left yesterday," Rachael said.

In the next few minutes they told each other of their families and what had been going on in the community the last few days. They knew Rachael had not been able to get out.

Rachael decided to go ahead and let them know what God had done for her. Most important they needed to know what Jesus meant to her. "Well ladies as you both know, I had not stopped working over at Ruthie's place, and you also know she is Mennonite. She shared Jesus Christ with me, and that is where my glow comes from, my beloved Savior. It says in the Bible in the Gospel of John 14:6-7, 'No one comes to the Father except through Me. If you had known Me, you would have known My Father also; and from now on you know Him and have seen Him.' Jesus told the people He was their way to salvation. It is all in the Bible, we only have to open it and all the information is in there," Rachael saw the fear on Rebeka's face for her reading the whole Bible. Martha's face on the other hand showed interest.

"We are saved through grace by faith in Jesus Christ." Rachael saw how Rebeka was drawing back and she wanted more than anything to share the Good News with her two best friends. "Now wait a moment. Before you start telling me that we are not to say we are saved, hear me out. We were bought and paid for by the blood of Jesus when He died on the cross for our sins. Yes, for each and every one of us," Rachael stated with a matter of fact tone.

"Rachael, that is a haughty thing to say, it goes against all we have been taught! And it is not in our beliefs! So why are you going on like this?" Rebeka could feel the heat in her face as she was more than just flustered.

"I am not trying to be haughty or anything close to that. What I am trying to do is what God tells me to do."

"Well, you sure do have the look of joy on your face. It does glow, which seems strange to me. What about your family? They will all be put under the Bann. How can you do that to your family like this? You know I love you like a sister, we have always been close; however, I do not understand your actions right now," Rebeka blurted.

Rachael reminded them that it would not be the kinner under the Bann, only Joseph, her parents, and herself.

Martha asked Rebeka to calm herself and let Rachael finish telling them what she felt in her heart. Martha had a softer countenance about her.

Rachel continued. "If you think I am happy because I have had such a wonderful life and that nothing ever happened to hurt or horrify me, you are wrong. I am happy because I have learned to let God take the injustice of all the betrayal and deceit out of me, and He taught me how to forgive."

"I've learned that my Heavenly Father cares for each hair on my head. He cares more about me than any human being ever could, and that my trust should be firmly placed in Him no matter what my problems or circumstances are. When you finally reach that level of trust in our Heavenly Father, and only then, can you stand strong in the face of your enemy and the most brutal of attacks. When the community finds out about my accepting Christ, the attacks will hit full force, but He will be there with me." Rachael said, "that is not to say I won't go through the Bann. However, with God and His Son beside me, I can get through anything." Rachael stopped to take in a breath and get some water down. Before anyone could say anything she held up her hand.

"Learning to have a personal relationship with Him is your pathway to forgiveness as well. He wants us to learn His Word and use it as our sword to fight the attacks of the devil. He wants us to share the love of Christ not with bitterness but with the love He demands we show one another." Rachael hoped she was not going faster than they could take it all in.

"Remember, we must learn to forgive in order to be forgiven. It is in the Lord's Prayer." Rachael realized she needed to calm down. She would not win her friends to Christ except to show the love of the Father. *Father please, help me.* She wanted to be that shining light for Christ.

"I didn't know all these things about the love God wants for us or the sacrifice He made for us, at least not until I started reading the whole English Bible. My cousin gave me a Bible to study with her. She couldn't have given me a better gift. We discussed at length what we studied. It didn't come easy for me to understand at first. The Amish are forbidden to enjoy and learn God's whole Word, just the parts we are to obey. So it leaves a lot to learn and understand. Before you judge me for what I have done, please take some time to pray and read the Gospel of John. When you have read it and prayed about all that is at stake here, then come so we can pray together. That is if you want to or feel God tugging at your heart." Rachael added, "Remember Rebeka, you said you would be there for me to the very end. If my personal relationship with Jesus puts an end to that, it will hurt me. It will tell me you are judging me, and remember it is only God's right to judge."

Martha and Rebeka hugged her gently. Martha said she would think and pray about it. However, Rebeka said she would not be going outside her faith and would pray for Rachael to repent.

At that point the ladies left, on the way out Rebeka looked at Martha shaking her head, and spoke. "Well, now you have someone to talk to about what you have read in the Bible. I have not forgotten that day we were in the kitchen and you told me you were reading on your own. You had better be careful or you will be under the Bann just like Rachael and Joseph will be." Rebeka spewed the words out. She knew she should keep her thoughts to herself. She decided to let it go at this point.

Anything further would only make Martha mad at her.

"Considering all the times you told me to lean on God, it seems you might be trying to serve two masters, and we both know that is not possible," Martha said cautiously. She did not want to say anything more that might drive Rebeka away.

As the days flew by Rachael watched her family one by one decide to accept Jesus as their Lord and Savior. Neither Joseph nor Rachael ever put any pressure on them to do so. Her heart felt so full of love she just knew it would spill over the top; she cried tears of joy in the privacy of her room. She didn't want anyone seeing her tears and thinking they were tears of pain instead of the joy. With God being at her side faithfully, her pain had subsided to some degree. She felt it was God and God alone allowing her the time she would need for Lucas and Paula's wedding. She praised God not only for the relief but it seemed He was giving her the extra time she had prayed so hard for. It would mean so much to her if she could be with them on their wedding day.

She thought throughout each day about her friends, Martha and Rebeka to see the joy she had found. She wanted them to see more of her so they could see for themselves. She prayed there would not be a division in the community church but a softening in the bishop's heart. Letting the People read the complete Bible and truly understanding how eternity is found.

Martha sent word she would be over within the next few days to visit. Martha said that as soon as school was out for Abby and Laura, they would have time for a lengthy visit. Rachael was praying to God Martha would open her heart to Jesus, which would be the best gift ever.

∞

Chapter 19

Laura wondered why things always seemed to go wrong in her life. No matter how hard she tried, she could not do anything right. She did everything they asked of her, even staying in school longer than the normal eighth grade. She wondered what more they wanted. *Well, at least Mamm didn't say anything to Daed about my walking Marty home the other night. Otherwise she would have been in real trouble.* It was not just her mamm's hurt look, which was bad enough, but if her daed had found out…. she just shuddered at the thought.

She felt they were treating her as if she were a bad person for being so anxious to start her rumschpringe. *We are allowed to do most everything we want during this period.* Ach, she did not want anyone to stop her from doing what every other teenager did. She was sure her parents had probably done things during their rumschpringe that she wanted to do now, and as far as she knew, they had never gotten into trouble. *Well, it will only be a couple days anyway and she could handle that.*

Abby saw no problem with the way things were going in their way of life. She always did what her parents and the elders asked of her. She felt good and had a great sense of peace when she did as the Lord directed. She just wanted to be a loving daughter, an obedient Amish girl, and of course a devoted friend. She had been praying for Laura, if only she could see how much better her life would be if she would have the same outlook. Laura just needed to look to God for all things.

Abby prayed. *Dear heavenly Father, help me to be strong, and show me how to help Laura. Please show me how to draw her back to You and the People. Help me to use wisdom in dealing with all situations that comes up, especially where those Englischer kids are concerned. Please put a hedge of protection around us, Amen.*

Abby decided to go over to visit Laura and see how things were going, but first she would let her mamm know. As Abby walked up the path to her house, her thoughts were of Laura, she had been kind of distant the last couple of times they had been together. She didn't blame her though, with all the changes they were going through. Just the thought their starting their rumschpringe within a few days is exciting and scary all at the same time. Laura didn't seem to be adjusting emotionally to the freedom they would soon be able to enjoy. Her attitude scared Abby as she thought about the trouble Laura could get into. Their rumschpringe period hadn't even begun and Laura already couldn't contain herself. Some of their young people didn't get through this period without getting into some kind of trouble. *We go from a life of self-sacrifice and discipline to total abandonment,* Abby thought.

As Abby walked into the house, she called for her mamm. "Mamm, are you in here? I want to go over to visit Laura."

Her mamm was in the living room and could hear Abby call.

"Abby, I am in here. Jah, you may go visit, but let me know if you are going any place else," Martha asked kindly. She knew she didn't need to worry about Abby, but Laura on the other hand is another story altogether.

"Ach, I will Mamm. I don't want to ever worry you like that again. I will be very careful about how involved I get with Laura's friends. I'll listen to the Lord and follow His Word." Abby hoped Laura had been praying for guidance from God in her life, she kept thinking to herself as she walked to the Knapp home. She certainly could hope couldn't she?

Lord, please help me to not live in a spirit of fear but of peace, joy, and a sound mind through You, Lord, Amen.

As Laura and Abby visited, they actually enjoyed their talk about their rumschpringe which would start in a couple days. It wasn't going to be a big event for either girl as they weren't going to receive any kind of certificate as it had only given them the two extra years, not a high school diploma. As Abby left, she said something to Laura that left her thinking about the position she was in with her family and with her heavenly Father. She said softly to her friend, "You don't want to burn your bridges with your family and especially not with God. So as soon as you start through your rumschpringe, please think about that. I love you very much." With that Abby bid Laura farewell and walked on home.

Abby met her mamm at the back door as she entered the house. She had been encouraged by Laura's reaction to her words, and told her mamm about her visit. She related all she had said to Laura to her Mamm.

Martha felt Abby's talk with Laura was well meant and she felt elated Laura was receptive enough to listen. However, Laura needed to be turned over to God, and Abby would have to realize this soon. She didn't want Abby getting into trouble trying to save her friend. *Abby has planted the seed*, now God would have to water it. Abby needed to let go and let God.

The next few days passed, finishing up the last of their schooling. Now both girls would be staying home learning what was needed to run a home and family.Laura started meeting her Englischer friends in town without Abby. Laura knew Abby didn't approve of them, especially Larry. Laura seemed to find him the most exciting of the group.

She was headed down the wrong path if she didn't change her ways. Talk in the small community ran rapid as Laura seemed to be the head topic of the conversation of the local Amish, who all thought Laura was on the wrong path. Abby had heard most of it, and it hurt her heart for her friend. She decided to try just once more to reach her. However, she decided to speak with her mamm first to get her advice.

After listening to her daughter's concerns, Martha decided she would try a new approach. "Abby, I wish with all my heart you would work on your own walk with the Lord." Martha hadn't told anyone yet about her own decision. "Allow God's plans for you to grow and see where it leads you. I believe God has something special in mind for you. Let God deal with Laura and her actions."

"I pray she will pick the right path," Abby said. "I love you so much for being such a gut mamm. I cherish our talks ya know; they are so special to me. And I love your wisdom. It must have taken a lifetime to learn what you have inside you. Not that you are old," Abby giggled, knowing her mamm would take it good naturedly, "but Mamm, if I can have any kind of gut influence on Laura, I feel inclined to go when I am invited." At that she turned toward the door.

Martha prayed. *Father, I turn the two girls over to You. They need Your protection. I am asking for a hedge of protection to stand strong against Satan's ploys. Give them wisdom to discern where it is coming from, from Satan or from You. I believe in my heart they are good girls. Just help them in their adolescent outings. I am not sure the Amish are doing the right thing by their kids, letting them run around and staying out until the wee hours of the night. There are too many temptations. I am not as scared for Abby, but Laura is another story. I am so grateful Abby reads Your Word, Amen.*

Martha spent many hours in prayer these days. She worried about Abby and Laura starting their rumschpringe. Then finding out about Rachael having cancer, she prayed nothing else would happen. How would she tell her family about her decision to follow Jesus? *There is only You I can turn to at the moment, please Father I am pleading with You to help all of us. Abby can be such a worry wart, she will be the hardest one to tell. With Abby's vivid imagination, she doesn't need to start worrying that her mamm might get sick from Rachael as well. But it would be public soon, and better Abby should hear it from her family than outsiders.* Martha found herself so caught up in her thoughts that she didn't hear Abby asking her a question.

"Mamm, did you hear me?"

"Ach, I am sorry daughter. What is on your mind?"

"I asked what lay so heavy on your heart? You seem a hundred miles away. I know it must be more than just Laura and me. Is that right?"

"Jah, I have something I need to tell you. Rachael is very sick with a terminal illness. I am so worried about her and her family." Martha stated sadly.

"Ach mei! Is she going to get better?" Abby asked with concern.

"No, my liewi, her disease is terminal and actually she doesn't have much time left here with us." Martha said as tears welled up and ran down her cheeks. Abby reached up and gently wiped the tears away.

"Mamm, are you for sure and for certain it is terminal?"

"Jah, your Aunt Rachael has cancer and sadly it is terminal. She doesn't have much time with us."

"Oh Mamm, that is horrible. How very sad! What about those doctors she has been seeing? Haven't they been treating her for months now?"

"Jah, she has been seeing doctors for months, but this is a disease that ravages the body; it is eating her body up. I'm sure you have noticed how much weight she has lost. We need to be strong for her and her whole family. They all of them need our prayers. You and Allie used to be so close, why don't you go see her? After all, Allie is your first cousin and could use a friend. That would give you a chance to visit with Aunt Rachael at the same time. I know I will be spending quite a bit of time over there until God takes her home."

"Mamm, how do you catch cancer? Will we get it from being around her?" Abby asked.

"That is exactly what I thought you would worry about. No, we can't catch it from her." Martha continued gently, "Cancer does not spread like a cold. We need to be thinking about how we can help Rachael and her family. The family will need a lot of help and support as her time draws to a close and she goes home to be with her Father in Heaven." Martha stated.

Martha felt relieved to see Abby was taking the news so well. She now had to tell the rest of the family.

Martha and Abby hugged each other as they rose from the table; they needed to finish their chores.

Abby went about her chores with a heavy heart. She was shocked at what her mamm had just told her. She could not believe Aunt Rachael was going to die. Abby wondered about the pain from the cancer. She prayed God would help her through this. She needed to be there for Marty and Allie. *Dear Lord, please show me what needs to be done, how to comfort my mamm, and how to be helpful to the Lapp family.* She remembered

Laura had said Marty had shared some family issues with her a few days back. *It must have been the cancer. Why didn't she tell me?*

Martha had been doing a lot of praying about her own relationship with Jesus. She would have to tell her own family about what she had learned from reading the chapters and verses Rachael had suggested to her. She felt sure she knew what she must do. *Oh Father, please give me the strength You gave Rachael when she came out with her news of accepting Christ as her Lord and Savior. The faith she put in You shows in the way she is handling her illness. Please continue to give her the peace that shows on her face.* Martha knew Rachel loved Jesus so much and couldn't imagine a life without Him. The peace she had found in His Word couldn't begin to explain the joy she felt in her heart. She must go see Rachael.

∞

Chapter 20

Martha had been spending time these past few days not only reading what Rachael had asked of her, but then when she had shared it with Aaron the previous evening, it became so much easier. She said a silent prayer thanking God that Aaron had been so open to listening to her. She gave much thought to John 3:16 "For God so loved the world He gave His only begotten Son, that whosoever believeth in Him will have everlasting life." Martha knew she would never have believed their Old Order could leave out something so important if she had not read it in the Bible for herself.

Why would they deceive the People? She felt deceived, and she had trusted their Old Order Amish ways and the bishop and preachers. Not only is she losing one of her best and dearest friends, but she learned she could not trust their leaders. She stood for a moment and felt so lost. Martha didn't know which way she should turn. She knew only herself and Aaron would go under the Bann, so it really wasn't putting her family under any risk in that situation? The fear of being shunned and put under the Bann didn't bother her so much; however, it did bothered her how it would affect Daniel. He was almost to the age of joining church. The rest of the family wouldn't be Banned. Actually, Daniel would be the only one old enough to have a say in his beliefs. The rest of the kinner were too young and would go with them.

She decided and knew accepting Jesus as her Lord and Savior was the right way, and the only path to take. She read and reread the Scriptures and continued on into the other books in the Bible. She always loved to read, unlike most Amish woman and had a mind of her own. Aaron had never given her a hard time about her reading. It had started when Aaron was in the hospital with a broken back. She sat with him day in and day out, but when he slept, she would pick up a book. Her reading is something she and Aaron had kept to themselves.

By reading the Bible, she knew in her heart that she must follow Jesus. However, her family's salvation must come first. The only way to Heaven is through Christ, so she felt she needed to ask God to help her and do just that. She and Aaron decided they too would accept Christ as their Lord and Savior. *Father, I am going to trust You, please be there for us.* She prayed silently as she readied herself to go see Rachael. She knew what she had read in the Bible, just not sure how to relate it to the children without further instruction. Maybe Rachael would be helpful with this.

She prayed Rebeka would be doing the same, reading the Scriptures. Now if she only came to the same conclusion that she and Rachael had, that would be another prayer answered, not only for her but for Rachael as well. With Rachael being married to her brother, that made her family as well, and she wanted to be there for her brother also. Martha knew she must keep praying for all involved.

Rebeka felt troubled the past few days, not only with Laura for being her testy self, but also with her lifelong friend, Rachael. *What is Rachael thinking? We cannot say we are saved. That is not our way. She and her family are going to be shunned, period.* She hated the thought of not being with her friend at this time when she is so frail, but she did not want to jeopardize her own family over this. Rachael should have realized what an awkward position she had put them in, she thought. She felt like going to Ruthie and asking her why, with Rachael so sick, would she convince her to leave the only faith Rachael had ever known.

Rebeka had a moment's reflection about the period in her life that she tried hard not to remember. If only Rachael would think back to when Rebeka's family almost went through the Bann, she might then think about the terrible time it was, not only for her, but her family and friends as well. *Oh Rachael, please don't go public with this,* she thought to herself. If Kathleen had not been willing to go through with their plan, she too would have been shunned and then Banned. *Oh, Rachael! Please don't do this.*

Rebeka knew in her heart that she would not actually go over to Ruthie's, however, she felt Ruthie to be responsible for the trouble that would take place here in the near future.

She read what Rachael asked of her. She felt the pocket-sized Bible Rachael had loaned her must have contained errors in it as their leaders would not have deceived them. They had been their leaders and mentors for as long as she could remember. She couldn't go against her church and put her family in a bad light.

As she pondered over the whole thing, she wondered how the meeting had gone between Rachael and Martha that day. They had agreed to meet again on this day. She really didn't want to be there. Even if what Martha had said to her was true, she was not as strong and just couldn't go against the church. *Besides, how could Martha stand there and tell me about serving two Masters?* Rebeka had known God all of her life. Besides, Martha was family to Rachael and it wouldn't be as noticeable.

She felt so torn, wanting Rachael to repent. She did feel convicted the last few days for her thoughts. It is as though something was tugging at her heart. *Is that just in my mind?* She hoped it was not dementia starting and she would not dwell on this any further. She knew she could not bring any of this up to Abraham or any other members of her family. That would be like opening a whole new can of worms.

Rebeka realized she would still be able to see Rachael a few more times unless it became public knowledge in their community. *Please God, help us all through this.* She knew she should tell Abraham, he is my husband and the father of my children, and the head of this house. *He is going to be upset with me when he finds out my knowing of the situation and not coming to him. Our bishop will take it out on him for not having control over his house. Our church is not going to put the Bann on right away. Well, not within the next few weeks anyway.* After that she would not be allowed to see Rachael again. *Oh my dear friend, how we don't want to lose you! God, what is right? Being bought up in the Old Order Amish, one did not go against the church.*

Rachael is so cheerful, Rebeka thought to herself. *With all that's on her plate, it just didn't seem normal to be that cheerful.* She wondered where the cheerfulness came from. Rebeka felt grateful Rachael had the support of her family and particularly her mamm, Sarah, who had always been a very strong woman. *That must be where Rachael gets her strength.* Rebeka had much to do before dinner would be ready and decided she best put all of today's thoughts aside for a time and get busy.

It hit her all at once. Ach mei, she realized she was acting like a self-centered teenager. My selfish thoughts have been about me. She was sounding like her willful daughter, Laura. *Oh God, please take this attitude from me. I need to be as helpful toward Rachael and her family as I can be. Lord, my daughter and her willfulness are out of control. Please help me help her. She needs to know going worldly will only bring her trouble and heartache and pain. If she only knew the pain she is going to have to endure if she goes worldly she might think again about it.*

Rebeka was not sure Laura would listen to her at this point, but she thought it was time for her to share some of her past, the child, and her older sister. She thought that if Laura knew of her past and the heartache it brought, she might see that her parents had her best interest at heart. As she stood at the sink preparing some vegetables to cut up, her inner voice said, *'Have faith, I am here for you.'*

∞

Chapter 21

Martha arrived that morning earlier than Rachael had expected. As she watched Martha coming up the walk she actually starting jogging the last part. The men had met her to take the horse and buggy into the barn. Rachel wondered what on earth is going on? Rachael made it to the back door just as Martha came busting through. "Martha, what is it? Is your family all right?" Rachael's frail face showed concern for her friend and sister-in-law.

"Ach, my family is fine. I am so thrilled I can barely contain myself," Martha said, laughing right out loud. "Ach Rachael, I shared with Aaron what took place over here when Rebeka and I came to visit last. At first, I couldn't help but be afraid he would not understand about your accepting Jesus as Lord and Savior and forbid me not to see you. I didn't know how to tell him I had done the same." Martha said with a huge smile.

"Martha, what did you just say?" Rachael could barely catch her breath. "Did you just tell me you accepted Christ into your heart? You told Aaron all this, and he wasn't upset?"

"He said God had been working on him as well, however, he didn't know what to do about it. He said something was tugging at his heart but didn't know why. He asked me to help him. I pinched myself just to make sure I had heard him correctly. I explained that the two of us should come here and speak with both you and Joseph. He didn't even hesitate. He agreed, and we will be over whatever night you think is best for your family. But you were right, God did tug at my heart. The feelings I have are truly amazing. The Bible seemed to be coming to life for me right on the pages as I read them. Is this some of the things that happened to you when you first accepted Christ?" Martha asked glowing.

"Martha! Ach Mei, Praise God! Are you telling me you are saved?" Rachael asked with tears streaming down her face. "And to answer your question, yes, there were many things that happened when I first came to saving grace."

"Jah, that's what I am telling you." Martha grabbed her friend. "Do you realize that now not only are we best friends, sisters-in-law, but now we are sisters in Jesus Christ?" She was laughing and crying tears of pure joy.

"God is good! Ach Martha, wait until Joseph hears about his little sister finding her salvation." That was all Rachel could say, her breath seemed to be gone from her.

"Rachael, are you all right?" Martha asked quite seriously.

"Jah, don't give it another thought." Rachael said as she eased herself onto her daybed. "It is almost too good to be true. You have no idea how hard I prayed these past few days. I finally turned it over to God. We are blessed with being able to turn our burdens over to Him. It is a huge weight lifted off my shoulders."

"We still need to be praying for Rebeka. I doubt she will be open to Jesus as her Lord and Savior at this point; there hasn't been one word from her since the two of you were here. I thought she still might come to visit as long as we are not under the Bann. But maybe she shared with Abraham and he forbade her to come. Again, I have to turn it over to God as it hurts my heart not seeing her too. Would you pray with me?" Rachael asked.

"Of course, my liewi, anytime," Martha hugged her more gently this time. "Rachael, Rebeka knew for some time that I had been reading more of the Bible, however, it wasn't until the day you shared your being saved with us that she reminded me I had told her a while back. I had forgotten until then. I am so grateful to have you in my life, for however long God gives me."

The two prayed for a while, and the rest of Rachael's family left them alone. Sarah had heard enough to know Jesus now lived in

Martha's heart and felt a warming in her heart for her. She lowered her head, smiling and giving praises to God for this wonderful outcome.

Rebeka had not gone over to see Rachael after she had told her about coming to saving grace. Rachael was sad for her friend, and she knew how hard it had been for Rebeka that day, and it would have to be in God's timing if Rebeka is going to find salvation. All she could do is to keep her in prayer. She did this throughout most days, she knew God told us to pray without ceasing, and when she couldn't think of a particular thing to pray about in her own house, she prayed for Rebeka.

Rachael and Joseph had faithfully been having a Bible study at their home led by Robert. Aaron and Martha were now coming too. They wanted to learn more before telling the rest of their family about the Good News of Jesus Christ. It is going hard on some of them, but it was wonderful to see the change in both Aaron and Martha. Each evening they had been able to have the study, then the two of them left arm in arm as if they were teens again. Rachael chuckled at the sight of them so much in love.

"What is so funny, my liewi?" Sarah asked her daughter as she helped clean up after the study.

"Ach mei Mamm, I can see the growth in Aaron and Martha each time we open our Bibles. Robert has a real gift for teaching each book in the Bible, he brings them to life and easy to understand. God has really blessed him with the gift of teaching. It does my heart good to see God watering the seeds. He is so faithful to those who seek Him out." Rachael shared with her mamm.

"I know this is the evening they chose to share with the kinner left at home about their new faith. It won't be long, and then it will be all over the community, by next week for sure and for certain. I have been expecting Joseph to be getting a visit from the bishop. Things get around here faster than gossip through the telephone lines when the operators listen in." Sarah chuckled.

"What do you think about the visit Joseph and Lucas are going to pay to the bishop tomorrow? Joseph said he might as well hit it head on as we now are stronger in our walk with Jesus and know He is with us. When God is for us, who can be against us?" Rachael asked with a grin.

"I believe he is doing the right thing. He will be there to be strong for Lucas. It is not as though Lucas will go under the Bann, so Joseph might come home with a lot of news for you. Do you think you are strong enough to take the news, no matter what it is?" Sarah asked.

"Jah, I will be just fine. You know these past few days I have felt a little stronger. I know you and the girls won't let me do much of anything, so I should not be tired; however, this is a different kind of feeling. I am not sure what is going on. Maybe it is just all God and He is making good on His promise," Rachael shared, "'I will never leave you nor forsake you. I will not give you more than you can bear'." Rachael looked to her mamm. "I pray to God for His will to be done, and I am ready for whatever He has for me." Rachael said more at ease than she had been since her family had learned the news of her illness. "Remember Stephen, the first martyr, who was stoned to death. The Holy Spirit came over him to help him through it."

"Maybe you should make a trip to the doctor and see what they think. They will be happy to know your pain has lessened. You aren't taking as much medication, and I feel this is God for sure and for certain. These doctors like to be the ones to tell you how you are to feel. They rarely think about how God fits into the equation and treatment of their patients. When do you think you might go in to see the doctors?" Sarah asked.

"I would like to wait at least another full week. I don't want to get any false hopes up. Does that make any sense? I would like you to keep this trip to the doctors between us for now. I do not want my family to worry until we see the doctors. They have had much to think about lately. That hunger you get for God's Word once you come to saving grace is a hunger you can't satisfy. I love to see them with their Bibles open and reading as fast as they can." "Once in a while there is a pause, like they are pondering the meaning. When they do have a question, I see them write it down as Robert suggested," Rachael said with a smile and a little shake of her head.

"Jah, they do have sheets of paper to show Robert when he arrives. It is funny to see them watching to see if they can get an answer before we start the study. Robert usually tells them he will answer the questions after the Bible study. He is so patient with them.

"Robert and Ruthie are wunderbaar gut friends as well as relatives. We are lucky to have them so close. I myself have questions for the next study," Sarah said to Rachael, she smiled and raised her eyebrows. She would wait until Robert was through with the study for the evening.

∞

Chapter 22

Martha and Aaron were going to have their hands full with all the kinner still left at home telling them the 'Good News' this evening.

All the kinner were there except Peter, he left to go to Ohio a couple of years earlier. On a visit out there, he met a girl he just knew would be the one for him, so he stayed. Martha remembered Peter saying, "Lily makes my heart go pitter patter." She and Aaron chuckled at the time, and then it hit them, he would not be coming home with them. Martha still missed him.

Lily's family had welcomed him in, however, they were Mennonite, and that had been hard for Martha to take. Peter had never joined church, so he didn't go under the Bann. Peter just started working on his instruction when they went to visit in Ohio, and when he met her, he could talk about nothing but Lily. There wasn't any way of talking him out of it either, so they left him there and went home.

They stayed in constant contact with him over the past two years. He seemed so happy, always bubbling with joy and laughter. It made it a little easier to have him back in Ohio knowing how happy he and Lily were. That is a mother's dream for her kids, no matter what they end up doing or where they end up living, their happiness is all that matters. In her heart of hearts, she believed Peter had already accepted Jesus into his. With those thoughts set aside, Martha turned to Aaron. They were almost home from Bible study, and she wanted to ask a couple of questions of him before they went inside to see the rest of the family.

"Aaron, wasn't that a wonderful study this evening? I feel like my eyes are finally opening. Like the scales are falling off as we learn. I can see why they say that when one asks Jesus into his heart, one gets a hunger for the Word of God that is unquenchable. I never feel full. I know I could not read any more than we do and understand what we read. The help from Robert, Ruthie, and even Rachael made it a lot easier to get through the Gospel of John. We are very blessed ya know, I think we are ready to share with the kids tonight. What do you think?" Martha asked.

"Jah, I reckon there is no time like the present. It is going to get around that the studies are going on each evening, and I want our kids to hear it from us instead of through gossip," Aaron agreed.

"Denki, I will feel much better getting it all out in the open. I also know we will have some problems with a couple of them. But you know something? Peter may be coming home when he learns about our leaving the Old Order. Ach mei Aaron, that would just be the best. Well, let's get ourselves into the house with the rest of the kinner and see how it goes. We will be saying a prayer and asking God for wisdom, right? Will you do that after we tell the kinner they need to listen for a while before they speak?"

"We will answer their questions after we get the Good News of Christ to them. I love you Aaron. You are the best husband any woman could ask for." Martha hugged his arm close to her and he bent his head and kissed her forehead.

Martha thought it would be hardest on her precious daughter, Abby. Abby and Laura had been best friends forever, Abby had even stayed in school longer with Laura. Martha would have liked to have had her at home as was the general rule with girls her age. Now she realized the damage it caused Laura going the extra two years.

It was over now and Abby's birthday had come and gone, however, she and Laura were staying in town way too much for her liking. She trusted her daughter; however, she didn't see much change in Laura's attitude. In fact, it seemed to be getting worse. She heard the girls argue at length several different times. This hurt her just to watch and she knew it hurt Abby; it was so unlike them to argue like that.

With Aaron and Martha telling the children of their new faith in Jesus, and if Laura's family still decided to have nothing to do with Rachael's family, she didn't know which direction Abby would take. She could only pray. Abby not being of age made her believe she would stick with them.

They needed to think about how Daniel would take the news. He always stayed so close to his family, however, she knew he found an Amish girl to court and didn't know which way he would go. She would have to leave him to God.

She prayed the kinner would follow Aaron and herself as Rachael's kinner had done. It would be something else to pray about. She loved the fact that she and Aaron had gone to the Bible studies over at Rachael's place. She had told the children they were going to visit Rachael, who would not be with them long, and to some degree that had been true. She felt better prepared to face her own kinner that night.

She had noticed a big improvement with Rachael though. She didn't seem to tire as quickly as she had at first. Martha decided she needed to let God do His will, but the extra strength gave Rachael the extra bit of stamina she needed to share her story with them as well as help Robert and Ruthie with the studies. They were learning so much now, but something still bothered her about the Amish leaving out big sections of the Bible. Maybe in Heaven she could ask God.

"Children, would you please all come to the kitchen table? Your mamm and I have some things to tell you," Aaron stated, "This is going to take some time, so if you want to get something to drink that would be fine."

The kids all looked worried and questions started flying from them almost all at once. "Is it Aunt Rachael?" Abby asked.

As the others started with their questions, Aaron put his hand up for silence. "Your mamm and I will explain when we are all gathered around the table. Now be patient with us. This is going to take a while."

The kids helped to get the drinks to the table and they all took their seats. Not interested in their drinks, they sat quietly looking from one parent to the other.

"Your Mamm asked me to start this conversation with a prayer to God. I am going to say it out loud and want you to bow your heads and listen with open hearts," Aaron said to his children. "Will you please do that for us?"

"Jah Daed, we want to hear it all," Daniel said.

Aaron started his prayer to God by thanking Him for His Son and for their new faith and their salvation. He thanked God for his family and asked God to help his children to open their ears to understand what they were going to hear. After saying, Amen Aaron looked up to see his kinner and the startled expressions on their faces.

"Children, your mamm and I have been going over to the Lapp home for the past few evenings so that we might acquire the knowledge to help you understand what it is God wants for all of us. I do not want to say anything bad about the Old Order Amish faith. However, the bishops decided to leave out very important parts of the Bible that we are to adhere to." Aaron paused, took a drink of his water, and continued. "Let's get our Bibles and come back to the table. I believe that it would be better for us to all read God's Word together and that way even the younger ones will be able to understand."

The children all left the table and went to fetch their Bibles as they had been instructed. It didn't take them long and were all seated and waiting for their daed to continue.

"Please open your Bibles to the Gospel of John." Aaron instructed. As he waited, he silently prayed to God to give him the wisdom he would need to get through this period. He wanted God's will to be done, not his. He finished his prayer, opened his eyes, and smiled at his kinner. "Well, let us turn to John 3:16 and begin there. We will go back to the first of the book later. There are a few verses your mamm and I have learned, and after that, we were able to make up our minds that we want to follow Jesus. Your mamm and I have decided that in reading the Bible, we now know that in order to be allowed into Heaven we must accept Jesus into our hearts and follow every Word God has for us. We want you first to read with us this evening and pray about it tonight before going to bed. That way, it will be God working on your heart, and it will be a decision that comes from you speaking with

Him." As Aaron went through the verses they had learned over at the Lapp house, he was careful to make sure his children knew that it had to be God's will being done, not theirs.

As the kids read with their parents through all the verses they had chosen, they were all very quiet, so quiet that Aaron and Martha began to worry.

Daniel was deep in thought. *Was this what their parents had been doing these past few evenings with Aunt Rachael and Uncle Joseph? What on earth were they thinking? Their parents would go under the Bann. That is what Aunt Rachael and Uncle Joseph and her parents will be facing too. Who is leading these false teachings?* These thoughts were running through Daniel's mind and he couldn't believe what he was hearing.

"Daniel, what is it, do you want to ask us a question?" Aaron looked at his son with love and concern. Daniel being the second to the oldest son Aaron didn't know for sure and for certain how Daniel would react to all this. He and Martha were pretty sure Daniel was courting a young Amish girl and that in its' self would cause problems if they were serious about each other.

"Daed, you and Mamm will be shunned from our Old Order and this is very serious. I do not want to lose you in my life, but I have been courting a young Amish girl and intend to marry her after joining church and going through the steps in getting there. What on earth are you thinking? I believe I am going to go to a friend's house and ask if I may spend the night with them. I have no intentions of living any other way but Old Order Amish. My girl is Amish as well as her family, and I am not sure I can be here right now. I am going to talk to the bishop tomorrow. I do not mean to be disrespectful, but I know the difference between what is right and wrong. I am not a child any more. The bishop is not going to look upon this situation any different than I do, good night." Daniel walked out the door and shut it a little harder than he meant to.

"Oh Aaron, what are we going to do?" Martha wrung her hands in frustration.

"We are going to leave it in God's hands, my *fraa. Du kann duscht (you cannot do)* anything with him at his age, except leave it up to God and pray." Aaron reassured his wife of many years.

Abby watched as the scene played out before her. She could not believe what had just transpired. *How will this affect my friendship with Laura? Will our parents still allow us to be friends?* She wondered if Rebeka and Abraham were doing the same thing, since Rebeka and Rachael had been her mamm's lifelong friends. *Ach mei, my mind is running wild with questions.* She needed to take a deep breath.

After watching Daniel leave the way he did, they then turned to Abby to see how she was dealing with the news. "Abby, are you all right?" Aaron asked.

"I can see by the look on your face that you are worrying about your friendship with Laura. I don't think you need to worry at this point. We will try to talk to Rebeka and Abraham if a problem arises. Will that ease your mind?" Martha asked.

Jah, I am worried about how this will affect our friendship. How will I be able to be with Laura when she is with those new friends of hers if I am forbidden to be with her? You remember the agreement we made?" Abby asked.

"What agreement did you make with our daughter that I know nothing about?" Aaron asked his wife.

"Well, my liewi, there are a lot that goes on with the boys that I am not privy to. And jah, I did make an agreement with our daughter. It is not anything for you to worry yourself over," Martha said kindly.

"I do trust you, you have always made gut choices throughout our marriage with our kinner. If you feel the need for counsel let me know," Aaron said softly.

"For now, Abby, I think you should continue on as you have been doing. I am still praying for Laura and that you will be a good influence on her. Besides, once we go into the Mennonite church, they have different programs for teens that are chaperoned. That way, there won't be the appearance of evil doings going on. We will talk more about this when the time comes." Martha patted the back of Abby's hand giving it a squeeze.

"Denki Mamm, that does ease my mind some," Abby sighed. "What is this going to mean for us in the Amish community?"

"All of you kinner will all be coming with your mamm and me to the Bible studies. That way, you will be learning right along with us each night. We have a lot of catching up to do and must forge ahead so that we might get caught up with your Aunt Rachael and Uncle Joseph and their family," Aaron said to his kinner.

Martha looked around the table to each of her kinner and with a reassuring smile said. "One thing for each of you to remember my little ones, you have not joined the church. Therefore, none of you will ever go under the Bann. You will be able to live here in this community and work and raise your own kinner. We want to stay here and watch our kinner grow and our kinskinner grow up as they come along." Martha opened her arms and one by one each of her kinner reached in for a loving embrace.

"What about Daniel? We don't want him leaving us." Abby said. "Besides we love him. Ach Mamm, what can we do about Daniel? He stormed out of here as angry as I have ever seen him in my lifetime."

"As I said earlier, we are going to turn the situation over to God," Aaron told his kinner with much love showing on his old, leathery, weathered face. "I would like each of you to read the Gospel of John and write down any questions you have so we can take them to the next Bible study. Robert and Ruthie have been such a big help to us. I am not sure we could press forward this fast without them. We are going to pray out loud from now on. 'For me and my house, we shall serve the Lord.' Let's end for tonight, and each of you pray on your own. I am very pleased with your reactions to the news we presented this evening. We truly understand it was a lot to take in. So off to bed with you," Aaron ordered.

After the kinner went to bed, Aaron tenderly held Martha's hand. He looked into her eyes that were so beautiful even after all the years. "God will lead and be with us to help our family."

"Aaron, I am so worried about Daniel. He is going to the bishop."

"We are going to let God deal with him, whatever he decides to do. If he goes to Bishop Malachi in the morning, like he said he would, we can expect to see Malachi here tomorrow. He will flip his lid over this. I just don't want it to affect Joseph and Rachael, she has enough to deal with. However, did you notice the extra strength she seemed to have this evening? It was nice to see her feeling better. I believe it must be God holding her up," Aaron said as he hugged his wife.

"Let's pray together before bed. God says where there are two or more, He hears our prayers," Martha said.

While praying and thanking God for being in their lives, they turned Daniel over to Him.

Abby prayed and fretted and stewed over the situation. She knew she shouldn't worry, but all she could think about is how this new relationship with Jesus is going to affect her friendship with Laura. Laura's daed is an elder in the church, and she knew Abraham Knapp would not take this news lightly. He for sure and for certain would not allow Laura over to their home after the Bann went into effect.

She also knew Daniel to be a person of his word and always had been. Therefore, she knew first thing in the morning he would be going over to see Bishop Malachi. She wondered where he would spend the night. He and Isaac had grown up together, but now were not all that close. He had been seeing someone for quite some time. She didn't know who, for she herself had not gone but to a few singings and Daniel hadn't been there. She had been so busy with Laura going into town that the singings were not on their schedule most of the time. All Laura could think about is going to town to hang out with those Englischer kids. Abby also knew Laura had gone to town several times without her, as word did get around in their small community.

She realized that because she would not be going to the Old Order Amish church services any longer, she would not see her friend except by going to town with her. She knew the Mennonites didn't have the rumschpringe period. They wanted to protect their teens from even the appearance of evil. It would be something to ask her mamm in the morning. Maybe she wouldn't be going to town with Laura any longer. She didn't even know if Laura would have anything to do with her or her family since they were affiliated with the group now going to the

Mennonite church. Only time would tell, and there wasn't that much time left.

So many things would be changing in her life. She knew Jesus; He had been living in her heart for a long time. He had been with her all this time, she just never thought about what it actually meant. The word *saved* had such a huge meaning. Oh, she prayed her friend Laura would try to understand. Her mamm had mentioned to her how the teens did things chaperoned, that is if they did end up there. The Mennonite kids were not allowed to run around at all. It would not bother her to be with kids who loved Jesus as she always had. She was sure it would be fun. She didn't think Laura would have the same view, though. Laura wanted that running around period in her life to be of her own rule, God's will was not in the picture at all. She fell asleep with a peace she just couldn't put into words.

Jon and Kenneth, who shared a room, were very close. They knew their parents knew what was best for them. The love their family had for one another would hold them together. They prayed for their older brooder, Daniel, who meant so much to both of them. They knew he was upset; however, surely he would come to understand they all needed him at home with them and would return. They didn't know about the kind of love a young man could have for a young lady. Of course they knew people got married, but how could that split a family up? Surely Daniel would not choose a girl over his family.

Karen and Sarah had been put to bed by Abby that night. She was so gut to them. She read them a story from the Bible as she had done so many nights of their lives. They loved their big sister with all their little hearts. They looked up to her and wanted to be just like her. Abby gave each a kiss on their foreheads and told them everything would be just fine. They trusted her as much as they loved her. Both girls snuggled down under the beautiful quilt and went to sleep.

Abby sat watching them sleep; she had been in their live from day one and felt as though she was another mamm to them. She also thought about what Allie was going through with Marty. The same thing ran through her mind how Allie would be taking over the role of a mamm to Marty. Even though their Mammi Sarah would be there for all of them, Abby would be the one they would turn to.

God was so good and she felt totally safe in His huge arms. Now having Jesus as her Lord and Savior peace engulfed her beyond words. *Thank You Father for giving us Your only begotten Son to die on the cross for all of our sins.*

Chapter 23

The next morning Daniel woke before dawn. He had not slept well in a strange bed, and thought how it nice it was of Josiah, Lisa's brother, to let him stay the night without a lot of questions. Josiah said a gut night's sleep would help him get his thoughts straight in his head. He had shared with Josiah just part of his dilemma, and Josiah had told him that going to talk to with the bishop would be the right thing to do.

Josiah knew Daniel was courting his younger sister. It is not normal for the siblings or parents to know about the courting of their kinner or siblings, however, Daniel's buggy had broken down one evening, and Josiah had come along and lent a helping hand in fixing the buggy.

Though Josiah was several years older than Lisa and newly married to Rachel, he didn't want to question his younger sister. It wasn't their way to be inquisitive about the rumschpringe. Josiah and Rachel had their own place, and he worked a blacksmith shop right there on the property, which had been doing quite well. He had learned the trade from an uncle, and it suited him perfectly. He loved working at home where he could pop in to see Rachel if he got the chance.

Rachel had coffee on the stove and it smelled so gut. Daniel made his way downstairs and into the kitchen. Rachel handed Daniel a cup. "Gut morning, Josiah went out to do the morning chores. He said you could give him a hand if you had a mind to," Rachel said with a warm smile.

"Jah, I do believe I will join him outside. Denki for the coffee and I want to thank both of you for the place to stay last night." Daniel offered with a smile of his own.

"Don't mention it. We will be here for you Daniel. Lisa thinks the world of you and she would want us to open our home to you. We are all so close in Josiah's family that it only seems right you should stay with us. So, make yourself right at home here and I will get breakfast going, it shouldn't take long." Rachel turned to get busy and Daniel let himself out the back door to find Josiah.

"Gut morning to ya, Josiah," Daniel said.

"Did you sleep well, my friend?" Josiah asked.

"Not so well. There are so many people involved that are going to be hurt. I have to think about my immediate family and then my Uncle Joseph and Aunt Rachael. I am having such a hard time with my parents' new beliefs. I don't know how to approach the bishop this morning except to just spill it all out. I feel bad being the one to turn my parents in; however, they are totally out of line by saying they are saved. They are praying right out loud and everything. I never thought it would be my parents that would do something like this." Daniel said with a heavy sign. He was very troubled by the turn of events in his life. The only thing he knew for sure and for certain, he loved Lisa more than he could even say and couldn't take the chance of losing her by changing his beliefs.

"I would not mind going with you if you would like. I have a small job to complete this morning right after breakfast. Mr. Knapp is coming by to pick up his buggy this morning, I have just one more strut to fix, and he will be on his way. He is not one for being idle, so I want to have it ready for him," Josiah said.

"I would be grateful if you didn't mention any of this to Mr. Knapp. I know his family is close to mine; however, I am not sure he knows anything about this. My mamm didn't say anything about Rebeka and Abraham joining in their Bible study. I wouldn't want to get things stirred up without knowing for sure he knew," Daniel stated.

"We are all a close knit community here in Lancaster County, and this kind of news will travel fast. I would not be surprised to find Mr.

Knapp knowing all about it. Seems hard to believe he would not know since his wife has been so close to your mamm and Rachael for all these years. Now if she shared the news with her husband, is truly another question. I guess a lot will come out today, not to mention this week. This is a church Sunday this weekend. I am sure we will get a lot of answers then as to who shows up and who does not. Let's get to these chores and into breakfast. Rachel is a gut cook. You will be pleasantly surprised." Josiah said with a big smile.

Rachel was as good a cook just as Josiah said. When they walked back into the house after chores, the smells from the kitchen made their stomachs growl. He enjoyed spending time with Josiah and Rachel, and his hopes were that he and Lisa would be married within a year or so. They talked about the need for someone to help at the Glick farm and Daniel hoped it would be him.

With both Jeremiah and Josiah owning their places, the time would be drawing near to when Mr. Glick would be in need of help. He had suffered from a fall he had taken during a barn raising. There were days his limp showed more than others. Lisa said his orneriness kept him going, but she always said it good naturedly. Having a community that stuck together and didn't expect outside help made them even closer. It had always been that way since the beginning of time. Well, his time anyway. At least as far back as Daniel could remember.

Breakfast being as good as it smelled he stuffed himself. Rachel insisted he take one more cinnamon roll. He patted his belly that stuck out and gave a little chuckle. "Rachel, I will be fat as a steer ready for butcher if you keep feeding me like this," Daniel said as he stood to get one more shot of coffee to wash down the last bit of his roll.

"As soon as you are ready to go see the bishop, let me know. I should be through in the shop with Mr. Knapp's buggy by then and we can be on our way," Josiah stated as he left for the shop.

"Josiah and I did discuss your living here with us. For the time being, we have plenty of room as we are not in the family way yet. We hope soon, however, there are plenty of bedrooms for now. So please make yourself comfortable with us," Rachel said kindly as she went about with her work.

"Denki Rachel. I do believe it is going to be hard to go back home. Even though the Bann won't go into effect for a few weeks, I feel betrayed by my parents. I don't want to stay there, and I can't thank you and Josiah enough, it means a lot to me" Daniel stated with a look of sorrow he couldn't hide.

At that he left headed for Josiah's shop. He met Mr. Knapp finishing up his business with Josiah and just leaving in his buggy. Mr. Knapp said good bye to Josiah and nodded at Daniel before taking his leave.

When they arrived at the bishop's place, they were pleased to find Malachi by himself.

"Bishop Strapp, would you have a few minutes for my friend Daniel? He needs to speak with you about a personal family matter." Josiah stated politely.

Malachi Strapp, a man who didn't mince words, looked over the top of his spectacles at the two young men standing before him. He recognized both as being in his district. "Jah. Come on in here and tell me what is on your mind, son."

Daniel followed the older gentleman into the barn. When Malachi turned around, he gave a nod of his head to sit on the bales of hay. He took one bale for himself. "Well young man, tell me what seems to be the problem this morning." Malachi looked at Daniel with one eyebrow raised.

Daniel didn't realize the pain in his heart would hurt to this extent. He loved his parents, but he knew the difference between right and wrong, and he felt for sure and for certain he was right in this matter.

"Bishop Malachi, I have brought news to you this morning that is hard in telling, but I know it is the right thing to do. My parents have been going over to my Uncle Joseph and Aunt Rachael's place in the evenings to study the Bible. Last night, they came home to tell us that they have accepted Jesus as Lord and Savior and that they are now saved. They know this is not our way; however, they said they would leave it up to God to deal with me. I want to stay in the Old Order Amish faith and want to marry one day. I didn't know what to do except come to you. I did tell my parents that I would be talking to you this morning, so it won't be a surprise to them when you go over to see them. I've been invited to stay with Josiah and Rachel for now. I am hoping with you talking to my family, they will repent and stop this nonsense." Daniel finished with a big sigh.

"I am glad you came to me, Daniel. Your parents have been in our church ever since I can remember. I am sure when I talk to them, we can work this out. They know all the rules, and some of their folks have gone through the Bann, so I believe they will come to their senses. That is the only way it can be. Where on earth did you say they were going for these studies?" Malachi asked sternly.

"Over at Uncle Joseph Lapp's place each evening for a while now," Daniel replied. "They said they are studying with Robert and Ruthie Lapp. Robert is our local vet and a gut one I might add. Uncle Joseph is my mamm's brooder. Ruthie is a cousin of Aunt Rachael's and has been quite influential over her since she worked for Ruthie. Of course, you know that Robert and Ruthie Lapp are Mennonites and always have been."

"Rachael has been awful sick here lately. She has dropped a lot of weight, and that is hard not to notice. Maybe they were just there to see her," Malachi said, hoping Daniel might be wrong. If not, the matter would put their community into a dither. Malachi thought as he reached up to pull on his long white beard. With Daniel shaking his head no, Malachi knew there was a lot more to this than a casual visit because Rachael was sick. He nodded his understanding to Daniel and rose to walk back to the buggy with them.

"Denki Bishop Malachi, I appreciate that you will help work this matter out," Daniel said.

Josiah and Daniel loaded back into the wagon and headed down the drive. They hadn't quite made it all the way out when a buggy turned to come down the Strapp lane. It was the Lapp buggy; Josiah recognized it, having worked on it before. "I wonder why they are coming here today. It is a work day. Maybe Rachael is sicker or something and in need of the bishop," Josiah said.

The Lapp buggy sat at the end of the lane waiting for them to pass. Joseph, a very friendly person, stopped to say hello. Josiah, always happy to see any of the People tried to strike up a conversation; however, he felt the tension coming from Daniel as did Joseph. Joseph wondered what had happened at the Stoltzfus place last night that Daniel would be with Josiah.

"Gut morning to ya. How are the two of ya today? Isn't it beautiful out this morning? A little cooler than it has been," Joseph said in passing.

"Jah, it is right nice out today for sure and for certain. You folks have a gut day now, you 'ear," Josiah said keeping his horse moving. He didn't want anyone getting riled up because matters might still work themselves out. Besides, he did work for Joseph Lapp, and that would not be good for his business.

They passed each other on their way. Lucas looked over to his father and asked. "Daed, do you suppose the bishop heard the news from Daniel, with his parents telling them about their being saved last night?"

"Well, if the bishop knows, it will make our job even easier. I am leaving it all up to God. We are not to worry or have fear. Let's put it in God's hands," Joseph said and gave his son a firm pat on the knee.

As Joseph and Lucas made their way down the lane, they prayed to God to give them the wisdom they would need to talk to their longtime friend and bishop. Joseph had known Bishop Malachi Strapp his whole life. Malachi was about twenty years his senior and Joseph didn't want to sever their ties if it could be helped. He had always cared for the bishop as he did all his neighbors.

They didn't want a division in the church; they just wanted to worship their Lord and Savior in the right way. And they believed that Jesus is "the Way, the Truth, and the Life." *Jesus tells us He is coming back for us and would not tell us if it were not so,* Joseph thought. *It is more important to my family and to me to have Jesus as our best friend. It tells us in the Bible not to follow man. Jesus tells us to follow Him. Please Jesus, give me the wisdom to speak with love and wisdom to Malachi that he may understand.*

∞

Chapter 24

Once Josiah and Daniel passed they arrived in a matter of a few minutes at the Strapp farm. Lucas took the horse and buggy to the shade of the barn. The bishop had watched them arriving and he waited to hear what they had to say. He didn't want a division in the church either, however, the rules were the rules. But he wanted to give Joseph a chance to speak first.

"Well, this is a nice surprise to see the two of ya here. Not working today? I hope Rachael is not any worse. Why don't you come on in the barn and I will have May bring us some refreshments."

May had been by the barn collecting the eggs and feeding the chickens. Being that close, she heard her father's request for refreshments. She took off to do exactly what her father asked of her without a moment's hesitation.

"Rachael seems to be a little better this morning, denki for asking," Joseph offered.

"What brings ya by today then?" Malachi asked.

"My wife and I decided that we would like to talk to you about our being saved before you hear it today by gossip. We have talked to all of our kinner, and they are going to stick with us. We are hoping that you will hear me out and also find the joy we have found. We have been friends for decades, and I for one do not want to lose your friendship. We are to love one another, as Jesus tells us to," Joseph said.

"Wait just a minute. What are you trying to tell me?" Malachi asked. He didn't want to let them know what he had learned just minutes earlier.

"Rachael's been cleaning for her cousin Ruthie Lapp for years to help us make ends meet. When Rachael became so sick, Ruthie still paid her to come, and they studied the Bible at Ruthie's so that Rachael would learn how important it is to have a personal relationship with Jesus." Joseph knew how hard this was for Malachi to hear. *God, please help me to say the right words so that Malachi will accept them as truth.*

Malachi sat there stone silent, just staring at the ground.

"Rachael started reading the whole Bible and read that when Jesus died on the cross for our sins, He washed us clean by His blood. When we asked Him into our hearts, ask forgiveness of our sins and repent, turning away from our sin, we then belong to the Kingdom of God, which also means we are saved." Joseph's voice had an assurance and calmness he knew came only from God. He knew the calmness couldn't have come from him. Joseph continued on, "We now have our names written in the Book of Life." "I just thought it best to come here in person before it got all over our community," Joseph stated.

Malachi was still being silent and when he looked up the sternness on his face said it all.

"We do know the rules of the Old Order and know what is in store for the adults in our house; however, please remember it will not affect the kinner, since they haven't joined church," Joseph said softly.

Malachi sat there shaking his head in disbelief, but didn't utter a word.

"We very much want to stay friends with all of you. I do understand that you have to do what you must. Just know that Rachael and I are always open to talk with you at any point. We have been friends for many years Malachi, and I would hate to see that change." Joseph felt he was rambling on, but Malachi still hadn't said anything.

"Lucas and Paula are going to be getting married here soon and would like you to officiate over their wedding. Lucas has never known another bishop, and we would like you to at least take it to God in prayer before making your decision." Joseph finished with a friendly smile.

"I can't abide in any of this. First, Daniel was here this morning to tell me that you and your family have been holding Bible studies in the evenings. Is this true?" Malachi now stood with his arms crossed.

"Jah, that would be true, we are reading the Bible with others. We are reading the whole Bible. God wants us to arm ourselves with His Word, our sword in times of battle. Most of the time that battle is against the enemy, Satan, and I believe that is what happened to the Old Order. Why else would you and the other bishops keep us from worshiping Jesus the way we are supposed to? He died for our sins, each and every one of us. Even you, Malachi," Joseph said with a gentle voice.

"Don't you go trying to tell me how to preach. Were you the one chosen to be head over the flock here in Lancaster County when the lots were cast?" Malachi asked with anger in his voice.

"It is not my wish to bring anger into this. My wife is very sick and she loves you. She would love it if for you to visit her. However, she also loves her Lord and Savior. Will you please read for yourself and then tell me why you and your pastors leave out the most important parts of the Bible. Please at least read The Gospel of John, all of it." Joseph added.

"Stop this nonsense now! I will not hear any more. I am ordering you to leave. You had better get your family to come to their senses and repent in the church before the People. You and your wife and her parents will go under the Bann in two weeks. Do I make myself clear on this?" Malachi was now yelling. "Do not come back here unless it is to tell me you are ready to repent. And to answer your question about the wedding, it is not the wedding season, and if they don't join church, I will have no part in marrying them." Malachi threw his hands in the air and yelled even louder, "Get out of here right now!"

May came with the refreshments at just that moment. She stood there with her mouth open, holding a tray of lemonade. She was afraid of her daed's wrath. She didn't like it when her daed got riled up. His face had turned bright red and she could tell he was having a hard time getting any air. Of late, even when he wasn't upset, just taking an ordinary breath was hard. His health had been going downhill for quite some time now. She worried over him and he wouldn't talk about his health with her at all.

"Sorry for the inconvenience, May. We'll be on our way. We feel bad for upsetting you, Bishop Malachi, please forgive us."

Joseph and Lucas left quietly. As they made their way to their buggy, they were both silent. They knew they must go home and tell Rachael the outcome of the visit, and Joseph didn't look forward to telling her anything that might upset her in her condition.

∞

Chapter 25

"Lucas, I am sorry that our meeting didn't go well. It is going to bring druwwel (trouble). However, God is in control. I am sure Robert will ask the pastor of his church to officiate over your wedding. Let's stop by Robert and Ruthie's place on our way home, we could use some prayer at the very least. It is a blessing you didn't join church, now you will be able to live in amongst the Old Order People and things should be fine. Your mamm is going to be happy for you no matter who marries you and Paula." Joseph smiled when he saw Robert's car in the driveway.

"We are almost to Robert and Ruthie's place. You can ask Robert to talk with their pastor and get this wedding scheduled as soon as possible. That would be one less thing for your mamm not to worry about. I know she says she leaves it all up to God, and we all know God is in control. I also know your mamm, she worries silently, or at least she used to.

"However, I do believe I see her in prayer more than the rest of us. But then she's had more practice at it while praying with Robert and Ruthie. She has changed so much in the past few weeks. I do know she has a softer countenance about her. She really is at peace, don't you think Lucas? God has done this for her, not any of us, it has not come from any of us," Joseph looked over at his son with a reassuring smile. "Everything will work out Lucas, don't worry son."

"I do see your mamm having a softer side than the rest of us. Daed, I feel good about Robert's pastor marrying Paula and me. Since we are not joining the Old Order Amish church, it actually will be better. The pastor will have our same beliefs. He will know the importance of our having that personal relationship with Christ. Malachi would only scoff at us, and I don't think any of us would like that."

They were coming up to Robert and Ruthie's and Robert came out to greet them. His first concern was for Rachael of course, however, after Joseph explained what had transpired with Bishop Malachi, Robert felt relieved and delighted all at the same time.

He and Ruthie had been praying their pastor would be asked to officiate over the wedding. "Oh, I am sure our pastor will be pleased if you would ask him. I am sure he would like to meet with Lucas and Paula as soon as possible before the wedding. For one, they are young, and two, he will want to know where they stand in their walk with Christ. I have told him about some of our Bible studies, and he is delighted. Would you like me to ask him to come to our study this evening?" Robert asked.

"Ach, that would be perfect," Lucas said. The excitement he felt at the news of Robert's pastor coming for the study that evening gave him an elated feeling. He also wanted to make sure Paula would be there. Not that she had missed a study since the unveiling of the news of her being saved.

"Daed, would you mind stopping over to the Miller place on our way home so I can make sure Paula will be there?" Lucas asked.

As they said their good-byes Joseph and Lucas were off to the Millers. Lucas sat fidgeting, he felt so nervous about getting Paula into difficulty with her Aunt Lisa and Uncle Robert. "What do you think, Daed? Do you believe the Millers will be all right with us getting married so soon?" Lucas asked.

"I think the Millers will understand. The Millers in Ohio are mostly Beachy Amish or Mennonite. Some of each, from what Robert shared with me. They also live in harmony together, even with some still being Old Order Amish. They allow each their own faith, and that is what we are praying will happen here. We love all of our neighbors; they have all been a part of our past for generations. We all go back a long time. I pray to God that He shows them that all we want is to love one another as children of God." Joseph sighed. He hoped Rachael would be strong enough for the news he would be bringing her.

"Daed, you are worried about Mamm. I can see it on your face. I am truly sorry we have bad news to take home to her. Maybe the wedding and meeting Robert's pastor will take away some of the pain from the Bann away." Lucas said softly, "After all, she is probably not going to see Rebeka any longer."

"Well, I pray you are right and this does not bring on so much pressure that she goes downhill faster. She has been doing so gut here lately." Joseph added.

"We'll be there for her, and you too Daed." Lucas put his arm around his daed's shoulder giving it a firm, but loving hug.

"There are a lot of different beliefs out there in the world, and as long as they stick to what is taught in the Bible, they too are children of God. Some try to add to or take away from the Bible, and that is where they get into trouble with God. We are to pray for them. God tells us to pray for our enemies. That is why I said we hope they will understand that it is each person's personal relationship with God and Jesus that matters," Joseph stated as they arrived at the Miller home.

Lisa and Paula both came out the door at the same time. "Is Rachael all right?" Lisa inquired.

"Jah, she is doing well this morning. We stopped to see if Paula might join us right after she helps you clean up the dinner dishes," Lucas being so excited, he could not wait to see Paula alone to tell her the good news.

"Why don't you take the rest of the day off from the chores around here my liewi, and go with them now. I can handle all there is to do here," Lisa said cheerfully. "After all, I won't have you here to help much longer with you and Lucas being married this fall." Lisa added.

Lucas looked at Paula; she hadn't shared their wedding plans with Lisa. Maybe the right time had not presented itself. "We don't want to take her away from her chores here with you, Lisa," Lucas stated. "However, today, there will be a lot happening in our community, so by day's end, I am sure you will have heard most of it. We might as well let you know now so that when Robert gets home, you can explain it to him."

"What is going on?" Lisa asked.

"Paula, do you want to share with Lisa what our new plans are?" Lucas asked gently.

"Joseph, would you explain to Lisa about our accepting Jesus, before I tell her of our wedding plans?" Paula asked.

After Joseph told Lisa about all the new changes and plans, he looked at her only to find her smiling from ear to ear.

Lisa took Joseph's arm and led him through the back door. Upon entering the kitchen, she turned and pointed to the sign that had always hung above the door. "But as for me and my house, we shall serve the Lord." Lisa gave Joseph time to read it and then said, "You see, my husband has always lived like that. The verse comes from Joshua 24:15. We will embrace your new relationship with Jesus, as we know we could not get by one day without Him in our lives. Now there will be more of us to fellowship with."

"Now Paula, what is it you want to tell me?" Lisa asked.

"Lisa, Lucas and I have been talking to his parents, and they are in favor of us going ahead to marry as soon as possible. With Rachael being so sick, we want to marry now so she will be there with us on our special day. Do you think Uncle Robert will be all right with this?" Paula asked.

"Your Uncle Robert will be delighted. Do you have a letter written to your family in Ohio? They will want to be here, you know that. The only thing is the celery is not quite ready. However, under the circumstances, I think all concerned will forgo the celery. We all love Rachael, and you are right, they gave her only a short time to be here with us, so I believe everyone will agree with your decision. I am so happy for you both. I am going to miss you and haven't had the chance to let you know I am in the family way again. I will have plenty of help here. Can you picture Alicia with little bobbelin to play with? It will be good for her to start learning to help with the babies. She is already a big help in the kitchen and with the household chores. We will be just fine. We will just miss that joy and spunk you have, though. Now be off, and give Rachael a hug and a kiss. Be sure to tell her how much she is loved," Lisa said as she scooted Paula toward the buggy. She stood there waving as the three of them made their way down the drive. Lisa knew Robert would be happy for Paula, as he loved her like a daughter. While she had lived with them, they had grown to love her as one of their own. They would miss her and that was for sure and for certain.

Joseph had been praying all the way home how not to upset Rachael. *Oh, what was he thinking? Well, there it is in a nutshell, he wasn't thinking. Rachael would be just fine; she had Jesus beside her.*

They entered the back door and on into the kitchen, Rachael stood standing at the stove stirring a big pot of *buhneuspp* (bean soup).

"What are you doing my fraa? (wife) We have three others here to do that. Where are they anyway?" Joseph asked a little frustrated to find Rachael up working with all the helpers she had.

"Ach Joseph, you are treating me as if one foot is already in the grave." Rachael laughed. "I am fine. I need to feel useful as much as I can. Now, please tell me all about the meeting with Bishop Malachi. Every part, don't leave anything out. Don't spare me, I am feeling stronger. I have Jesus right beside me, don't ever forget that." She knew it hadn't gone well. It was written all over their faces.

"Paula, I am so glad you came back with them. We are always blessed to have your smiling face here."

"Denki Rachael. Being here is my heart's desire. Well, that desire is right behind God and His will for me." Paula chuckled. "I don't seem to get the right words to come out when I am around Lucas." Again she giggled, and she pulled Lucas by the hand.

"Malachi actually ran us off, he sure did," Joseph said. "Is that enough? I don't believe I need to go into details now."

"We will have to pray for him. Did you let him know we would always have our door open to him?" Rachael asked.

"Jah, I did. Lucas had a good thought about the whole situation though. I have to agree with him too," Joseph stated.

"What thought? Don't keep me in the dark," Rachael said. "Start from the beginning."

"We arrived right after Daniel had been there. He had told the bishop about our Bible studies, so Malachi was armed and ready. He asked me if it were true, and I told him it was. I shared our story, praying the whole time he would be open to at least part of it. No chance there. When I told him we were saved, I thought he was going to drop dead in his tracks. His face got all red. We didn't even get to have the lemonade May had fetched for us. He ordered us off his property. He told me not to come back unless I was ready to repent. It is sad to see a fine man like that so deceived. He told us he would have nothing to do with the wedding either. He told me I had two weeks to get my family in order or the Bann would go into effect."

"Ach, you did have quite the meeting, didn't you?" Rachael stated.

"After we left, Lucas and I thought about Robert's pastor officiating over the wedding. So we stopped and asked Robert if he would ask his pastor. As God would have it, Robert agreed to not only ask him, but he is coming to the Bible study this evening. Robert said Pastor Holmstead would want to meet Lucas and Paula. He wants to know how far along they are in their walk with Christ," Joseph stated. "So we had better have extra refreshments for this evening. He will be bringing his whole family."

"You know, my mamm and our girls have already started making goodies for this evening." Rachael patted Joseph's hand.

"We then went to make sure Paula could be here this evening, and Lisa told her to come with us now. So, here we are," Joseph told her.

Rachael thought he looked like the same as he had when she had married him many years ago. His hair was all tousled from his hat and he stood there with his hands turned up.

"To our surprise, Mamm, Lisa told us that she and Robert are also saved. What a morning! She showed us the sign that hangs over their kitchen door. It turned out to be wonderful news. Lisa told us she was so happy now that they would have more people to fellowship with." Lucas and Paula were grinning from ear to ear.

Rachael was confused. "You mean to tell me that Lisa and Robert are Christians? They moved here and joined church? I don't understand."

"Lisa told us they always lived in and amongst the Amish in Ohio and wanted to do the same here. Besides, she said it was better for business. They kept their faith to themselves. Personally, I am not sure I could do that. I have such a love for my Savior I want to shout it to everyone I meet." Joseph's voice bellowed love.

"Ach, this is wunderbaar gut news. And if they choose to keep it under their roof, that is their business. At least that won't keep them from coming to the wedding. After Robert and Lisa think about it for a while, I am sure they will join

them even if they do lose business from a few Old Order folk," Rachael reassured everyone. "Paula, be sure to let them know they are always welcome to join us for Bible studies when they are ready." Rachael said with hope on her face.

"You are right as usual, my fraa. I am not sure why I was afraid this would upset you. You always seem to be able to find the positive in most things. Even your illness doesn't seem to get you down in spirit." Joseph gave her a sweet smile. It had always made her heart beat faster.

"Abby will be coming this evening to Bible study, Allie," Rachael said to her daughter as she came into the kitchen to help her Mamm. Allie gave her mamm a gentle hug, said hello to Paula, and then asked if she might take over for her.

"Allie, my thoughts are for you to get Abby to open up a little about her feelings. You are just six months older, and even if you haven't been as close to her for the past two years since she and Laura stayed in school, that is probably all going to change. I doubt Abby will choose to hang out with Laura if Laura doesn't change her ways," Rachael offered.

"You are right, Mamm," Allie said with a sweet smile.

"Abby is not too happy with the way things are going between her and Laura. Would you do that for her please? And you being here for the studies will help her, so let her sit by you. That way, she can see how you take notes. It makes it a lot easier to write down the verses Robert makes reference to and look them up later. Maybe after the study, you can go back over them with her. When God and Jesus say something several times, they do it because they want us to get it. It means it is very important," Rachael said to her eldest daughter.

"Oh Mamm, I have missed Abby so much. It is not that I wanted to go on in school. It is my friendship with Abby and Laura I missed. But Laura was always so caught up in herself." Allie pondered what she had said for a moment. "I am sorry I said that. It wasn't nice of me. I am going to pray for her. I truly am sorry I said something about her that wasn't nice. I believe it says that when we do that, it is like we are killing them. Not by the sword but with our mouths," Allie said. She prayed, *God, please forgive me.*

"Allie, I am so proud of the spirit that lives in you. When you do something you know is wrong, you humble yourself and ask forgiveness right then. I believe that is what you did when you closed your eyes briefly, am I right? It is the Holy Spirit that lives in you, He does a right gut job of convicting us. Does He not?" Rachael gave her daughter a big hug and kissed her soft check.

"Jah Mamm, that is exactly what I did. However, once I am upstairs before bed in my prayer closet, I will be on my face before God truly asking forgiveness."

"Right now though, I do believe that daybed looks inviting. Even though I am feeling stronger, I don't want to run out of steam this evening at Bible study."

Rachael said as she walked into the sitzschtupp (living room).

"Would you like me to bring you something to drink, Mamm?" Allie asked.

"I think we all could use something. Your daed and Lucas had quite a visit with Bishop Malachi. You were out back when they came in. I am not going to go into anything. Just know that we have been given two weeks to repent in front of the People in the Old Order or the Bann goes into effect. We have nothing to worry about though, because we have God." Pastor Holmstead is going to come this evening to the study and I am sure he will be bringing his family this evening. Would you make sure there are plenty of refreshments to go around after the meeting?" Rachael asked.

"Sure Mamm. It will be fun to have all those folks here, including the Holmstead family with us this evening and worshiping together." Allie said. "And I am looking forward to Abby being here too.

Remember, when you and Martha used to get tongue-tied over calling us? '*Abby!* I mean *Allie!*' and the other way around was always so funny." All laughed out loud for the first time in a while.

The house had gotten too serious for Rachael. She smiled at the sound of the laughter. She knew Allie had been carrying a lot on her shoulders without so much as a whimper. She found herself feeling very blessed. *Father, I thank You for giving me such a loving, obedient daughter.*

Joseph came to sit by his wife and hold her hand gently. He did so as if he were afraid she would break. He shook his head unconsciously. "What is it, Joseph?" Rachael asked.

"Ach, I just can't express the love I see flow from you. You are truly amazing. You seem to not be in as much pain, are you?" Joseph asked.

"Not really. There are times, but it does seem to be less. I am not sure what is happening, and do not want to give you any false hopes, but I am going to go see the doctors this next week. I didn't want to worry you, so I didn't mention it. I don't know what they are going to tell me, however, I am not going to let them forget that God is a big part of the equation, either way it turns out. Please don't be upset with me for not telling you of my appointment. You have had so much on your mind. I didn't want there to be one more thing, especially when we can do nothing about it. But God can," Rachael said, looking sheepish.

"I am not giving up on you. And I am not giving up on God. Look what He has done for this family in the past few weeks. It has been amazing; our whole family has accepted Christ as Lord and Savior. The tears flowed with each child. I could not hold them back. I felt so blessed to be married to the most amazing woman I know and to have loving children who truly care for one another as well as for others. You have done a remarkable job raising our children," Joseph said with love in his eyes.

"My dear husband, it has been both of us, we made the decisions together. My mamm has been a wonderful example to them also. Can you believe it? My mamm was saved for years and didn't tell a soul. I guess for some, it is very personal. For me, I am like you. I wanted to jump up on any roof top available and scream it to the whole world. I think Lisa and Robert have been like my mamm. The Beachy Amish group they came from is more progressive than most. I was surprised when they came here and the letter came from their bishop in Ohio that Bishop Malachi allowed them to join us. Listen to me. I said 'us'," Rachael laughed. "You see, I still feel part of them. And that is what God tells us to do, love thy neighbors as we would love ourselves. What part of that don't they get? That is an order from God. We may not always agree on things, however, what they do is between them and God, not us. Therefore, I pray we all will go on treating them as though nothing has happened. I am still going to say hello even if I get no reply. That way, I know I will be doing what God wants me too," Rachael said.

"I am going out to help the boys and let you rest." Joseph kissed her forehead as he left.

Rachael laid her head down and closed her eyes. She was just going to rest for a few minute. The next thing she knew, she was awakened by a call for dinner. Ach, she had slept two full hours.

"Rachael, do you want me to bring dinner in here for you?" Sarah asked.

"No thank you, I am joining you at the table. I had a great nap, and now it is time I am up and helping. Ach, this looks great. The four of you do a fine job of putting on a wunderbaar gut spread. Absolutely everything looks good. And the smells, I have a hard time believing I slept through those smells. Let's get seated." Rachael cheerfully sat down waiting for the others.

Joseph led them in prayer; he had them all hold hands. He asked if anyone else wanted to give thanks. Rachael said a short prayer of thanksgiving. The rest were quiet as they were not yet accustomed to praying out loud. Joseph assured them that it would come in time. He shared with them that at first, he had tripped over his tongue. They all laughed, thinking of his tongue sticking out so far that he was falling over it. He was a tall, lanky man, and the kinner laughed at the thought of his tongue hitting the floor and it made them all laughed heartily.

He shared his testimony with them while they ate. Tears welled up in some of their eyes as they thought of the stern daed they had always known turning to mush in a matter of speaking. He is so much softer, and the love just flowed from him. The house is filled with joy; they were all beaming with the love of Christ in their hearts.

"Daed, do you think we can make one of those signs that Robert and Lisa have in their kitchen?" Lucas asked.

"What sign?" Rachael wanted to know.

Paula had seen the sign so many times. It had not dawned on her until today the true meaning it had in the Miller home. She hoped Lisa would help her write the letter that had to go out tomorrow to her parents and other family members in Ohio.

"As I said earlier, Lisa led us into her kitchen and pointed to a sign above the kitchen door. She said it had always hung there. It says, "But as for me and my house, we shall serve the Lord," Joseph said. "I guess there could be several ways to take those words. She said for her and Robert, it was Jesus and always had been. She also shared it was from Joshua 24:15."

"It probably was a smart thing to keep it under their roof. Mamm has done that for years, keeping her faith in Jesus Christ secret, except from my daed, of course. They knew the consequences if they came forward. It is like what happened to the Jews in Germany when Hitler decided it illegal to worship. They sometimes only had a few pages of the Bible at a time to study. And if caught, it was worse than being shunned, they were murdered. What a monster Hitler was, makes me shudder," Rachael said.

"Instead of taking care of their elderly like we do, Hitler ordered all the useless eaters, the old folk, (gray haired people) out to the edge of town and shot them. On that note, I think we need something sweet. Let's have a few cookies and get our minds focused back on God and how lucky we are to be able to worship Him in the open," Rachael stated. She hated what Hitler had done to God's chosen people during the Holocaust. She didn't understand how this happened to God's chosen people with Him being in control. She prayed she would be able to ask God when she got to Heaven.

Allie brought a plate of cookies and placed them on the table. Rachael thanked her daughter squeezing her around her waist.

"One day, that will change. That is in the book of Revelation. But before we get there, we will study the book of Daniel. Robert said that Daniel is a prelude to Revelation, that it puts Revelation in the right prospective. In the book of Daniel it is broken down into seventy weeks, and sixty nine of those weeks are prophesied, they are finished. The last week is all about the tribulation period. We have a lot to study before we get that far in the Bible. Not to change the subject, however, I am still full from that gut dinner, so just one cookie will sweeten us up a little. Denki to all you ladies for all you do," Rachael said, looking around the table.

"You need not thank any of us. We do it for our household and friends because we love doing it in the name of Christ," Sarah said.

"I want you to know that with each one of you coming to saving grace these past two weeks have lifted my spirits to the highest. I will rest in the Lord now, I feel ready if it be God's will," Rachael said softly.

"Let's all pray it is God's will that you will be with us longer than those doctors said," Lucas stated, "We are going to plan the wedding as soon as Pastor Holmstead has met with us and gives us his blessings. If the meeting goes well, can we make the wedding for the next off Sunday for the Old Order?"

"My thoughts exactly, to hold it on an off Amish Sunday is a wunderbaar gut idea. That way, those who want to come from the Amish church can come and not be missed. It would be too obvious otherwise who was absent and only cause them more problems," Joseph stated. "If we had it weekend after next, it would give Paula's family time to get here. We are praying they all come. I bet you are anxious to see your family, right Paula? I believe that when we went to visit out there in Ohio, your parents, Peter and Mary, were the only two Millers we missed meeting. How will they feel about you marrying a non-Amish man?" Joseph added.

"My parents are progressive Beachy Amish, and in some of my last letters to my mamm seemed as though she wanted to tell me something. They also have that same plaque Robert and Lisa have above their kitchen door. But until today, I had never given it much thought. Makes me wonder if they have been worshiping Jesus the way Uncle Robert and Aunt Lisa have been doing. Please help me keep them in prayer," Paula shared, "I feel so blessed to be marrying Lucas. I already love all of you. You already seem like family to me and I feel so blessed."

"We already feel you are part of our family too, and of course we will help you pray for your family. I can't wait to meet them, especially your mamm," Rachael said with her face aglow with love.

"The sooner the wedding takes place, the happier I will be. I not only want to be a gut wife for Lucas, but I want to help you here, Rachael. I already feel like you are another mamm to me. Thank you for inviting me into your family, all of you." Paula squeezed Lucas' hand. She smiled a loving smile at her betrothed.

"Ach mei Paula, you are giving up a lot to not have a big wedding. Are you sure this will be all right with you?" Rachael asked.

"Jah, it will be just fine with me. God knows how much I love Lucas, and He also knows how much I love Him. Being married by a pastor of our same faith makes it perfect," Paula smiled from ear to ear.

"We seem to have just enough time to finish up the chores before everyone should be arriving," Joseph said getting up and heading out the door with Lucas and the other boys in tow.

∞

Chapter 26

Aaron and Martha had been expecting Bishop Malachi, and true to his word, he showed up. He would not come into the house; he took Aaron to the barn. The barn is where most of the meetings between the brethren were held anyway. He told Aaron his son had been by to visit him that morning and had told him everything. He looked Aaron straight in the eyes and asked if the things Daniel had told him was true.

"Malachi, if I did nothing else right, I did teach my children to always tell the truth. I am not going to deny my Lord and Savior. Does that answer your question?" Aaron asked, looking at Malachi with kindness. If he couldn't show him anything else, Aaron wanted him to see the love of Christ through him. As Joseph had done, he told Malachi their door would always be open to him.

"I am going to tell you just as I told Joseph, you have two weeks to get your house in order, get the family to church for them to repent, or they also will go under the Bann. Do you understand?" Malachi said harshly. "Do you and your study group know this is going to tear our community apart?"

"Only if you let it Malachi, we don't want a split in the church. We only want to do as God tells us to do, love thy neighbors as we would love ourselves and pray for our enemies. We do not want to be enemies in the community. We want our kinner to live here with us, and they will all be out and amongst you. Please Malachi, try to seek God in this before you go any further. I believe if you would open your heart, you would see how wonderful it is to live amongst true believers in Christ.

It is not some cult we are going into. We just want to study all of God's Word. One thing that comes to mind right now is you must forgive to be forgiven. That also goes for you, Malachi. I only say these things to you because we all love you and want you to be a part of our lives, here and in Heaven. Please pray about it, and come back before the two weeks are up and let's pray together," Aaron encouraged.

Malachi stomped off toward his buggy. He was so angry he felt there must be steam coming from his ears. He had not been able to get a word in edgewise with Aaron. *Well, let them rot in hell. We don't need them in our Old Order anyway.* He was almost to his buggy when he remembered that he had told Daniel he would let his parents know where he was staying. "Aaron, Daniel is going to stay with Josiah until you and your family comes to your senses. At least that young man has not lost his mind." With that Malachi got into his buggy and off he went.

Aaron and Martha hugged each other. Aaron shared with his wife the anger that had spewed from Malachi's mouth. "I now see that there is spiritual warfare that goes on right here on earth. Well, with Satan having rule over earth until Christ's return, it's no wonder." Aaron thought it had to have been the devil himself speaking. He told Martha he let Bishop Malachi know their door would always be open. The response he got didn't surprise him in the least. It just saddened his heart.

At least they knew Daniel would be staying in a good home. Josiah and Rachel Glick were nice folk. Josiah had been the blacksmith in the area for some time now and was doing quite well. They would pray for Daniel and not force him to come home. They knew the Glick families were upstanding folks, all of them. They had been friends, even going to the same church.

"I am sure that Malachi will have a sermon to beat all sermons this coming Sunday. It will be all hellfire and brimstone. I am sure the love of God will not be shining that day. Malachi is feeling threatened by those of us studying the Bible, and with two families involved, he figures there will be more to follow. Martha, please do not let this bother you," Aaron said.

"We thought we lost Peter to us two years ago when he stayed in Ohio. However, I believe you are right in your thinking. He married a nice Mennonite girl and didn't want to live Amish at all. Now with that letter you sent him, he knows we are not Old Order any more. Maybe he will start wanting to come home for a visit. That is my prayer for all of us. With Daniel being so young, one never knows what God's will is for him. Look at us, my liewi, would you have ever thought even six months ago we would be changing direction with our walk? Actually, we didn't have a walk with Jesus six months ago." Aaron hugged Martha.

"This evening after the study, maybe the brethren can discuss which church we will attend. We do need to be in fellowship at a church. Pastor Holmstead seems to be a nice gentleman," Martha said. "He is Robert and Ruthie's pastor at the Mennonite Church," Martha offered.

"Jah, I am sure Pastor Holmstead would be a gut person to help us get our own church started. Like the Beachy Amish or one like that. We might talk it over like you mentioned," Aaron said, pulling on his beard.

"Aaron, let's share this evening with the group what Daniel has done. I am sure Joseph got an earful this morning. Didn't you tell me Bishop Malachi said Joseph had been over to see him after Daniel was there?" Martha asked.

"Jah, he waited to let Joseph speak to see what he had to say, and then he let him have it. Joseph was the first one of us Malachi told about the Bann. Joseph tried to talk to him as we are supposed to do. His offer that their door would always be open to him at any time didn't do any good." Aaron said.

"I hope when Joseph got home and reported to Rachael the outcome of the meeting, it didn't upset her too much," Martha stated kindly.

Aaron went out to help the boys finish up, they still needed to grab a bite to eat and head over for the Bible study. He knew that as soon as they were through with the Gospel of John, it would be a weekly Bible study. This would be a period of time for them to catch up with the rest of them.

When the men came back in from finishing up the chores, the horse and buggy sat hitched in the barn waiting for them. Aaron knew they didn't have much time and didn't want to waste any.

As they sat for their dinner meal Martha could tell all the kinner was nervous about going to their first Bible study. "Abby, with us going over to Aunt Rachael's place for the study, Allie will be there for you to begin getting reacquainted with. I am sure she is looking forward to seeing you. The two of you need to get close again as you were before. You three girls were always together. This will be nice for you to be around a young woman who loves the Lord. We want to stay living Plain just like before, so that won't change anything. The only reason we have that phone down by the end of our lane is purely for emergencies because of all the accidents at the crossings. With us being the closest, I do believe it is a necessity," Martha stated.

After they finished eating their meal, Martha and Abby quickly washed up their dinner dishes and put them away. Then they were on their way to the Bible study.

Martha remembered saying a silent prayer as she had put the last dish into the cupboard. She wanted Abby to stop going to town and hanging with those Englischer kids. She prayed for them too. She knew Abby would make the right choice with God's help.

∞

Chapter 27

On the ride over to the Lapp place, no one uttered a word. They were all thinking about the events of the day. They all felt something missing. It was not something, it was someone. Daniel being a huge part of the family, and the oldest brooder living at home would be missed beyond words. He was usually outspoken about most things, not that he wanted to be disrespectful to his parents or for that matter, not to his siblings either. They all loved each other and did most things together. They all knew that they would be praying for him to come home.

As they drove the buggy up to the Lapp barn, they were met by Jonas and John. Both boys greeted them and asked if they could stable the horse. The two boys were so cute, and they seemed as happy as clams. Jonas is growing into a fine young man. Jonas was only a few years older than John, it seemed as though they were attached at the hip being as close as they were. Both were cotton tops like so many in their area.

Martha often wondered if Rachael thought of the twins she had lost and what they would have looked like now. She knew the twins were with the Lord. That was one thing she didn't understand why babies died, *they are so innocent*. The other being why her friend Rachael would die so soon. Maybe one day in Heaven that would be a question she would ask.

"Denki boys, for helping your parents out like you do. That would be right kind of you to unhitch and stable the horse. You are expecting a few more to join us this evening if I remember right." Aaron offered a warm smile.

"Mamm and Daed asked us to have you come in as soon as you got here. There is a matter they wish to discuss with both of you before the others start arriving," Jonas stated.

"Well then, I guess we better get ourselves inside. We will leave Jon and Kenneth with you, and they can help you this evening. Abby, Karen and Sarah can find Allie and help her and Marty get the refreshments redd up," Aaron said.

As the boys watched Uncle Aaron and Aunt Martha head for the house, Jon and Kenneth asked how different it is for them with the new belief. When Jonas and John explained it really wasn't any different, just more joyful each day, the other two boys seemed more at ease. At that the boys took the horse into the barn after parking the buggy off to the side where the others would soon arrive.

Aaron and Martha entered the house and were cheerfully met by Joseph and Rachael along with Joseph and Sarah Ingersol. They were all standing in the kitchen waiting on their arrival.

"Come, let's have a seat here at the table, we wanted to know what your thoughts are about us getting into a church, and which one. We thought of the Beachy Amish for one. Do you have any input on the subject?" Joseph asked as he led them to the table.

"We were speaking about the same thing earlier. We thought the brethren in our circle could have a meeting with Pastor Holmstead. He might have some suggestions. We don't have anyone to lead the church at the moment. We might see if any other churches have an upcoming pastor that is ready to step forward in ministry. If only Bishop Malachi would understand how important it is to have that relationship with Jesus, we could stay together with all the People we grew up with."

"Well, we know now after his visit with me, we won't be going in that direction," Aaron said. "After all, I believe the Holy Spirit can't be there if Jesus isn't accepted as Lord and Savior. I think that is called a dead church. Sad, isn't it? We are to keep them in constant prayer."

"I don't think it matters as long as we have a personal relationship with Jesus and stay strong in our walk with Him where we go to church,"

Joseph stated. "I have also read some about the nondenominational churches. Then there is always the possibility of our joining with the Mennonite Church Pastor Holmstead is over. Robert and Ruthie are happy going there. Robert told Rachael the teachings were very good, that Pastor Holmstead lets God lead him. I think that is important for the pastor to wait on God for answers. I just know the Old Order is so very staunch in their beliefs and won't budge an inch in their readings in the High German Bible. No one will ever tell me I can't worship Jesus. I for one will not let anyone tell me I cannot pray to Jesus, He is our Savior."

"I believe the same way. I am positive Pastor Holmstead won't push anything on us we are not ready to embrace. They will be showing up any moment. There is also a Conservative Amish Mennonite we might consider. Let us take it to God in prayer after the study this evening. I know at some point, Pastor Holmstead is going to speak with Lucas and Paula about officiating over their wedding, that is if he feels they are ready." Rachael humbly offered.

In just a few minutes the back door opened, and the people started filing in. *Ach, God is so gut,* Rachael thought. She hugged each as they came by. She welcomed them with open arms. It is going to *be wonderful to have more to fellowship with.*

"Good evening to all of you," Pastor Holmstead said. He went about introducing his family to everyone. He put his arm around his wife and said with much affection, "This is Edna." His children stepped forward and the Pastor went about with those introductions. "This is my eldest daughter, Esther, and her husband, Earnest, and next is eldest son, Samuel," He smiled warmly at the two youngest "this is Edgar and my daughter, Suzi. We loved being asked to join your study this evening. Shall we do a quick introduction around the room and get started?" Each daed made introductions and took their seats.

"Robert asked me to start this evening's study. I believe we will begin with prayer, then songs of worship for our God and Savior," Pastor Holmstead began almost immediately.

After the worship he said, "Now I am going to ask Robert to come up and continue where he left off with you last evening."

"Please turn to the Gospel of John and turn to chapter 12. Let's begin in verse 25. I just want to read this again so it sticks with you. "The man who loves his life will lose it, while the man who hates his life in this world will keep it for eternal life." And 12:26 "If anyone serves Me let him follow Me; and where I am, there My servant will be also. If anyone serves Me, Him My Father will honor." Robert paused allowing this to sink in. "This is just one more place where Jesus tells us we must follow Him. This is a command; it is for those of us who want eternal life anyway. I know I do, how about all of you?"

"I do," Rachael spoke up. Then she smiled at the group, "Being so sick has made me open my eyes to what God wants in my life. I do not want to spend eternity with Satan, and I doubt any of you do either. Excuse me, Robert. I didn't mean to get carried away there," she offered very meekly.

"No Rachael, please do not be sorry. You hit the nail right on the head," Robert stated.

As the night progressed, Robert went through the rest of chapter 12. He did it slowly so that the new ones joining the group could take notes. It pleased him to see the ones who had been coming for a while helping the new believers.

As they finished up with their study, he asked if there was anyone who felt God tugging at their hearts to give their lives to Christ. There wasn't anyone who spoke up that night, so he prayed for any that might still be lost and then closed with a prayer.

"I understand there is to be a wedding soon. Would that be you, Lucas?" Pastor Holmstead asked with pleasantness about him. "We can step out onto the porch. Would that be all right with you and Paula?"

Lucas looked to Paula, she nodded yes, and Lucas agreed.

The three of them made their way out to where a few benches sat on the porch and took a seat. Pastor Holmstead asked if they could be on first name basis and for them to please call him Michael. He said he is not one to stand on formality. Only Jesus deserved to be held that high.

They thanked him and told Michael about how they had come to saving grace. Michael had been especially thrilled by the elderly woman who had shared with Paula on the bus ride to Lancaster County. He thought to himself, *God works everywhere*. He listened for about an hour as the two young people told him their heart's desires. What pleased him most is that they both wanted God to be front and center in their lives and their marriage. By that time he gave them his blessings agreeing to marry them the Sunday after next.

When the three entered the house, they were met with lots of questions. Many cheers went up. Rachael could not contain herself. She welled up with a few tears and gave God His due.

They had now come to the end of the evening and before the group dismissed themselves they asked Michael his opinion about a church.

"It seems to me that you folks should agree upon your church. It is not about a religion. It is about a personal relationship with Jesus Christ. So is it that important to have a name? Why don't you come with Robert and Ruthie and see if our church might be the home church you are looking for? Seems some of you have been enjoying Robert's teachings, we do the same in our church. One only needs the Bible to teach out of. It is all in there, I feel safe staying straight with God that way. If I am to understand you correctly, this is what you find important, that the whole Word of God be taught, is that right?" Michael asked. He hoped this lovely God fearing group would join them. He would leave it to God to work on their hearts.

"I believe my family and I will be joining Robert and Ruthie on Sunday," Joseph said. "If it had not been for them, today I would still be blind."

"I feel the same way. Martha said it well the other evening, 'It is like scales falling from my eyes," Aaron said looking at his wife smiling. "So I guess we will also be joining you."

In that they all gave thanks to God for their new church family. It really is wonderful to fellowship with other true believers. They agreed to meet the next evening to continue their studies.

Allie came to Abby telling her how happy she is that they had joined them. "Please, let's stay close. I have missed you so much. I am glad to have had these last two years with my mamm instead of continuing on in school. However, I am glad you had the chance for more education. I'm just not sure it was necessary for our way of life, at least not for me."

"I am not sure it was either. Once you go into the high school books, things get worldlier. They want to teach kids about all these modern things, making them want them. I can't say that happened to me, but I worry about Laura. Will you help me keep her in prayer?" Abby asked.

Allie told her she had already been praying for Laura and would continue to do so.

The group agreed that once they were through the Gospel of John, they would meet once during the middle of the week and then of course on Sundays. After their good-byes, they left for home.

Abby sat in the middle of her brooders with Sara sitting on her lap all the way home. Karen sat on her mamm's lap. She wanted to protect them from the world. She knew she didn't want her mamm sending them on in school. Her thoughts went to Laura. *What a difference it had been to be with Allie this evening. Allie glowed. Even with her mamm being so sick, you could see Christ's love through Allie. She is soft, humble, a true treasure to be around again. Laura didn't really care what anyone thought of her actions. Didn't she know God saw all things?* She knew Laura would not stand to be preached to. All she could do for Laura was to pray for her.

She knew Allie would pray for Laura too. When Allie asked about Laura, Abby felt embarrassed to remember some of the things she had witnessed from Laura. She hated the thought she had been involved at all. The presence of evil showed in all they were involved in. That was the same feelings she had each time they were with those Englischers kids. Ach Laura, she didn't want to lose her friendship. However, she knew she didn't want to hang out with those kinds of kids any longer. *Ach mei, they even tried to make Laura steal that one night. And the other nights, ach, she hoped no one would find out she had been with them. Father, I am so sorry. Please forgive me, my heart is so heavy with sorrow.* She prayed silently giving Sara who sat on her lap a hug. She got a big smile from her little sister.

∞

Chapter 28

The Sunday meeting was held at the Abraham Knapp place. Malachi arrived early, He wanted to get the backing from Abraham. He was not going to let this congregation tell him what was what. The other pastors had met with him several times, and they each thought he would be doing the right thing. Malachi needed to set this group on their heels, making them see the Old Order way is the right way, the only way into Heaven.

"Morning Abraham, did you give thought to my question?" Malachi asked.

"Sure did Bishop Malachi, my family will be staying with you in the Old Order. We would not leave just because of two families. They say they see some light for crying out loud. I say they turned on the electricity. Know what I mean?" Abraham said with a shake of his head.

"Jah, I think you are right. We have always stuck together, but I fear this will tear this community apart. I heard about a story once, where this congregation parted. They took a chain saw and actually cut the building in two, right down the middle. The group that did it, they took their half across town. It seemed a funny story then, but now that something like that is crossing our path, it isn't so funny. Not that we worship in any building," Malachi said.

"I am going to let them know today they are not to go to that wedding," Malachi continued, "Why, it isn't even the season for it."

"I can't believe that Robert and Lisa Miller would allow Paula to go ahead and marry that Lapp boy. What are they thinking? You don't think they are going to get involved, do you?" Malachi was on a roll.

"Well, I would sure hate to see it happen. I know he gets a lot of his business from us. He would be losing a lot by going the wrong way," Abraham said, letting his eyebrows rise.

The other buggies and wagons filled with benches for church started arriving. It sure pleased Malachi to see so many of them. It had to mean he still had control over more of the community than he had thought.

The men got the benches set up and the podium placed up front for the bishop. After Pastor Levi Stoltz led them in morning prayer, Pastor Jeremiah led them in song. Bishop Malachi waited for a few minutes for things to quiet down, and then stood up. He walked to the podium and looked out at the congregation. He slowly walked around the room, pausing to look at each face. He thought he had their attention now.

Bishop Malachi gave a shorter sermon than usual. He was so filled with anger that it was obvious to Robert and Lisa Miller that Satan had gotten his foot in Malachi's door for sure and for certain.

"I am going to talk to you this morning about an issue that has raised its ugly head in our midst. Two families have decided to leave the Old Order Amish. I gave them two weeks to come back and repent. These two families have let Satan get a hold of them. We all know we will have to stand before God on Judgment Day, each on his own merit. We have to show God our works and our righteous standing. I feel sorry for them, however, I only gave those two families two weeks to come to their senses or the Bann will be placed upon them." Malachi stalled for a moment, again scanning the group.

"There is to be a wedding next week and none of you are to go. I would like to speak to Robert and Lisa Miller after the service. This is going to tear us apart unless we stand united." At that second his fist hit the podium almost knocking it over. His face was blood red with anger. He took a few minutes to gather his thoughts, still looking around the room. Not one person dared to breathe. They did not want the wrath of Malachi coming down on their heads. This was not unusual for the bishops to get angry over some of the people leaving the Old Order Amish Church.

"You are all dismissed now. Robert, will you and Lisa step up, I need a word with you," Malachi said. "We will sit down in just a few minutes to the fine spread I am sure the womenfolk have redd up for us."

"Malachi, why are you singling my wife and me out this morning? Have we done something to offend anyone in our congregation?" Robert asked right out. He wasn't going to let Malachi jump on his wife. After all, his house is his responsibility, and they did worship God and Jesus. They just didn't say anything in public.

"I want to know why you or your wife didn't come to me the minute you heard Paula would be joining Lucas and his family? Wasn't this Amish girl put under your protection? Robert, what on earth are you going to tell your brooder, Paula's daed?"

"Well, I thought I would leave that up to God. We invited them to stay with us and attend their daughter's wedding. Bishop Malachi, you have to remember, these families are not under the Bann yet. So I can't see how you can tell us we can't go to the wedding." Robert stood firm.

"You go to that wedding and just see what happens to you," Malachi said in a voice very similar to that of a dictator Robert thought of.

"Bishop Malachi, we don't want to lose any of you as friends, however, my wife and our family will be attending that wedding. Paula is like a daughter to us, and she didn't joined church. Therefore, you can't treat these young people, who only want to love their Lord and Savior, like they were criminals," Robert stated as a matter of fact. Robert took Lisa's hand and led her away before Malachi could attack her also.

"Robert, do you think we should get our kinner and go home for our meal? It sure would not feel very comfortable to eat in and amongst people who are going to look down their noses at us. I am sure the kinner are feeling the same pressures we are," Lisa said softly, "Let's go Robert, I for sure and for certain do not feel comfortable here. Maybe Bishop Malachi will calm down for the sake of the others." Lisa said taking her husband's arm.

"Jah, I do believe we will go. I don't feel the Holy Spirit here with these people anyway. I want to fellowship with true believers who have the Holy Spirit living in them," Robert said.

Robert gathered the kinner, and Lisa decided not to bother with the dish she had brought for the common meal. It wasn't worth it. On their ride home, she and Robert decided right then and there they would be joining Joseph and Rachael and those who loved Jesus.

"We have a wedding to plan for, and I am sure that some of Paula's family from Ohio is already on their way. I am sure that between Rachael's and Martha's families, we will be able to put up as many as show up. We sure want them to feel welcome. I know that Paula shared in her letter with her mamm about giving her life to Jesus. Paula said when she got the return letter yesterday; it was full of love and happiness for the young couple." Lisa shared with Robert.

"I want our boys, especially Micah and Jacob, to help with the wedding. We don't have much time, and I did speak to Paula. She thought she would ask Allie to be her bridesmaid as well as Abby. So that leaves Micah and Jacob to stand up with Lucas. This is different than we have been doing for weddings; however, I am sure Edna Holmstead will help us plan everything. With her husband, Michael, marrying them, Edna would be the one to ask for help," Lisa seemed to be thinking out loud as her mind raced.

"Rachael would like to do more; however, it wears her out to do too much. She said the other day how blessed she felt just to be able to go to the wedding. She said she knew it was God holding her up, carrying her when needed. She smiled so sweetly when she shared that with me."

"Paula also reminded me about the plaque that is above the kitchen door in her parent's house in Ohio. She said it is exactly like ours. She said since I shared that we also have Jesus in our hearts and have just loved Him silently, that she felt her parents were doing the same thing, it is in her mamm's latest letter." Lisa beamed with delight.

∞

Epilogue

Join us in book two as all involved are anxiously awaiting the upcoming wedding.

Bishop Malachi is going around the county telling all he sees not to attend. He is trying to hold his Old Order Amish together with a tight fist, and after the last Sunday service, he could tell Robert and Lisa Miller would be joining the other group.

Laura can't believe her daed told her she would not be going to the wedding and neither would their family.

Mary tried figuring out a way to go to the wedding and be with Micah. After all, she loves Paula, and besides she had known Lucas all their lives.

Rachael didn't know what to think, she is feeling stronger. She thought maybe God was giving her more time so she could make it through the wedding. Accepting Jesus into her heart has given her such a feeling of peace. The only thing better is that was her whole family now had done the same.

Will Laura and Abby still remain friends, or does Laura continue on with her outings with the Englischer friends? Abby knew she had to keep her friend in prayer. She wants God's will to be done for not only her but for Laura also.

God had been so gut to her and since giving her live to Christ asking Him to come live in her heart forever. She knew now a personal relationship with Jesus was worth way more to her now than a night out on the town. Please forgive me God for my rebellious attitude, even if it was only trying to protect her friend.

Family Members in Book One

Abraham and Rebeka (Ebersol) Knapp
    Isaac, Mary, Laura, Jonas, Mark, and Debra
Joseph and Rachael (Ingersol) Lapp
    Lucas, Jonas, Allie, John, Marty, and deceased twins
Aaron and Martha (Lapp) Stoltzfus
    Peter, Daniel, Abby, Jon, Karen, Kenneth, and Sarah
Robert and Ruthie (Zook) Lapp
    Robbie and Ginnie
Bishop Malachi Strapp
    May
Robert and Lisa Miller
    Thomas, Ethan, Alicia and upcoming twins
Micah Miller, Jacob Yoder, and Paula Miller all living with Robert Miller
Moses and Edna Glick
    Jeramiah, Josiah and Rachel, and Lisa
Pastor Michael and Edna Holmstead
    Ester and Earnest, Samuel, Edgar, and Suzi

Amish Glossary

ach—oh
alt—old
Ausbund—a hymnal
Bann---no one is allowed to speak to the person or persons, they are not allowed to attend the Old Order church, they are to sit at a corner table to eat by themselves. The rest of the family are to look right through them as though they are not there.
begreiflich—easy
bobbeli—baby
bobbelin---more than two or more bobbeli
bohnensuppe—bean soup
Christenpflicht—a book of prayer
dabber schpring—run quick
daadi—grandfather
daadi haus—grandfather's house. (Refers to an add on to the main house for grandparents to live in their elderly years.)
daed—dad or father
dankes—thanks
denki—thanks
die—the
do—here
druwwel—trouble
du—you
du bischt—you are
du kannscht or du kann duscht—you cannot do
dummkopp -- blockhead or dunce

duscht—do
ehrlich—honest
Englischer—a non-Amish speaking person. Some conservative Mennonite sects are not considered Englischers.
entsetzlich—awful
es—it
fraa—wife or woman
grossmammi—grandmother
gut—good
hatt—difficult
haus—house
hullo---hello
ich—I
im—contraction (in the)
iss—is
jah---yes
kapp—prayer covering cap
kinner—children
kinskinner—grandchildren
liewe—dear or sweetheart
mamm—mom or mother
mammi—shortened term of endearment for grandmother
mei—my
net—not
People—Amish name for their sect or group
Plain—Amish name that sometimes goes with People, like Plain People
redd up—make ready
rumschpringe—running around period for sixteen and older
shun---the pre period of the Bann
sich—yourself
sitzschtupp—living room
verschteh—understand
wunderbaar—wonderful
wunnerlich—strange
ya—yes

Made in the USA
San Bernardino, CA
03 May 2015